P9-DNF-659

ANGLEBERGER

# TO KICK A CORPSE

## THE QWIKPICK PAPERS

Books by Tom Angleberger

In the Qwikpick Papers series
*Poop Fountain!*
*The Rat with the Human Face*
*To Kick a Corpse*

In the Origami Yoda series
*The Strange Case of Origami Yoda*
*Darth Paper Strikes Back*
*The Secret of the Fortune Wookiee*
*Art2-D2's Guide to Folding and Doodling*
*The Surprise Attack of Jabba the Puppett*
*Princess Labelmaker to the Rescue!*
*Emperor Pickletine Rides the Bus*

In the Inspector Flytrap series
*Inspector Flytrap*
*Inspector Flytrap in The President's Mane Is Missing*

*Fake Mustache*

*Horton Halfpott*

For younger readers
*McToad Mows Tiny Island*

# TO KICK A CORPSE

## THE QWIKPICK PAPERS

Found by
## TOM ANGLEBERGER

Amulet Books
New York

An important note to the reader
from Tom Angleberger

What you're about to read is the third—and last—bundle of papers from a box full of notes by some kids that was found at the old Qwikpick gas station in Crickenburg. I am pretty sure they're from 2000. Things were a LOT different back then. These kids didn't have cell phones. They couldn't just run Google Maps if they got lost or call their parents if something bad happened to them.

Another big difference is in Crickenburg itself. Back in 2000, developers were building town houses and strip malls everywhere ... except in the downtown area, which was emptying. (Because everyone was moving to the town houses and strip malls.)

And one of the biggest differences is to Greenhill Plantation, which is where the kids go to kick the corpse. Now it has been fully restored, and every kid in the area has been there on a field trip at least three times. But back in 2000 it really was empty and falling apart. And as for the local legend about the standing-up corpse in the plantation tomb? They're still telling that story and even selling postcards about it. But the people who run the plantation don't know the whole story. And since they probably won't read this book, they never will. But you and I will.

Tom Angleberger

# THE QWIKPICK PAPERS

The official report of The Qwikpick
Adventure Society and our noble journey to
kick a dead person

## The Qwikpick

# SECTION I
## Introduction

This is the official report of The Qwikpick Adventure Society and our noble journey to kick a dead person.

If you have read one of our previous reports--and you probably should NOT have read them, because even though they are official, they are also confidential--but if you did read one, you may be wondering how this report could exist, since The Qwikpick Adventure Society was officially disbanded after the disastrous ending of our search for the Rat with the Human Face.

If you have NOT read one of our previous reports, you are probably wondering what The Qwikpick Adventure Society is. (And you're definitely wondering why this was typed on a typewriter, I'm sure.)

And either way, you are probably wondering why we would want to kick a dead person.

We're going to answer each of those
questions quickly so we can start the
report:

## WHAT IS THE QWIKPICK ADVENTURE SOCIETY?

The Qwikpick Adventure Society is
three people: Marilla, Dave, and Lyle
(me).
We picked that name because we meet
at a place called the Qwikpick.
The Qwikpick is actually Qwikpick
#8, the gas station/convenience store/
biscuit place on South Franklin Street
here in Crickenburg. Lots and lots
of people come through the Qwikpick
all the time to get gas, coffee, and
biscuits. Biscuits are a big deal here,
but they don't have anything to do with
this story, so I'll skip them for now.
Anyway, all these people come
through the Qwikpick, but they don't
realize that the Qwikpick has a second
floor. That's because it started out sort
of like a house and the gas station was

next to it, and over the years they sort of grew together. Larry, the manager, used to live here when it was still sort of a house, and a bunch of his old junk is still up on the second floor in the employee break room.

We are basically the only people who use the employee break room, even though we are not employees (obviously, since we are still in middle school).

But my parents are employees, and I (Lyle) was hanging out there all the time anyway when Dave and Marilla started hanging out with me.

The break room has all this weird junk:

(A) a record player

(B) a box of old records

(C) a speaker that says "Positive Energy" on it

(D) an almost-working TV (gets only channel seven from Roanoke)

(E) a ton of old videos from when the Qwikpick used to rent videos

But even with all that cool stuff
in there, we did eventually get sort
of bored just hanging around inside
all the time.

So we decided to have an adventure.

Now in books and movies and stuff,
people usually don't just decide to
have an adventure. Instead, they get
tangled up in a big adventure by
accident. And then after they defeat
the criminal masterminds or arrest
the smugglers or kill the orcs, they
go back to having a normal life.

Well, none of those things happen
around here so we had to make
an adventure happen. Our first
adventure was sneaking into a sewage
treatment plant, and I think the
moral to that story is pretty clear:
"Don't Sneak into a Sewage Treatment
Plant." I won't go into the details of
how bad it smelled here--just refer
to official report #1 of The Qwikpick
Adventure Society, Sections X-XV.

Our second adventure was the
search for the Rat with the Human

Face, and while we did find the rat,
we also got into such huge trouble that
Marilla's parents said she could never
go on another adventure again and
she couldn't even go to the Qwikpick
again or even talk to me anymore. (She
was allowed to talk to Dave, which was
totally unfair, but if I get into that,
I'll never get to the next part.)

So, basically, that was the end of
The Qwikpick Adventure Society, because
Marilla was really the leader because
she was the one who always talked me
and Dave into doing stuff.

**IF THAT WAS THE END OF THE QWIKPICK
ADVENTURE SOCIETY, THEN HOW CAN THERE
BE A THIRD ADVENTURE?**

Remember how Marilla was the one who
always talked us into doing stuff?

Well, she thought of something that
she wanted to do SO bad, she was willing
to break her parents' new rules and
risk gigantic, earth-shaking levels of
trouble.

What did she want to do so bad?

Kick a dead guy.

And she wanted to do it so bad that she actually talked me and Dave into wanting to do it too.

Now that those questions are answered you may be wondering why we wanted to kick a dead person.

We'll explain all that in Section II.

And if you're wondering if we really DID kick a dead person, that is what this whole official report is all about. So you can either skip to Section XXIV or you can just keep reading.

And the reason it's typed on a typewriter is not because I still don't have a computer. I now have a computer! It just doesn't work. So THAT'S the reason why this is being typed on a typewriter.

UNOFFICIAL Personal Note

I didn't want to bog down the official report with this story, but here it is. Skip it if you want to find out about kicking the dead guy sooner.

Dave and I chipped in $25 each to buy an OLD computer at the thrift store to use here in the Qwikpick break room.

The thrift store really isn't that far away (it's basically behind Taco Bell, but by car you have to go past Hardee's and turn there to get into the parking lot. Dave and I just walked through the field behind the trailer park and then cut across the Taco Bell parking lot, so like I said it isn't that far), so we decided we would just carry it home. The computer was heavy, but the monitor was HEAVVVVVVVVY and hard to get a grip on and you could barely see where you were walking when you were carrying it . . . Dave dropped it in the field  and it busted. It was sort of my fault since I said, "WATCH OUT FOR THAT COW PIE!" even though there wasn't one.

So I was mad at him for dropping it and he was mad at me for allegedly causing him to drop it, so we were mad at each other for a while, but now we're saving up to get a new one. (We only need the monitor since the computer made it to the break room safely and seems to be fine. It makes the right sort of noises when you turn it on—you just can't see what it's saying.)

## SECTION II
## The Punishment

Okay, to find out why Marilla wanted to kick a dead guy so much, we need to go back a bit.

If you read official report #2, you know that things ended badly. Really badly.

After Marilla's parents made us stop being The Qwikpick Adventure Society, Marilla had to face the Punishment.

First of all, she was grounded for two months. And trust me, I know from personal experience that when you live in a trailer, getting grounded is ROUGH. There's nowhere to go or even move around. It's like being a prisoner . . . and Marilla's got it bad because her cellmate is her little sister Neveah, who never ever does anything but watch The Lion King.

A while back they came out with The Lion King 2 and Marilla thought at least there would finally be something new to watch. And Marilla even kind of enjoyed it, but her sister hated it and stopped it in the middle and went right back to watching <u>The Lion King 1</u> again.

Plus, the grounding included Marilla having to miss being in the Spring Concert, which is a really big deal if you're in the school band because it's all anyone talks about for the entire spring.

The Scene of the Punishment: Marilla's trailer.

The grounding finally ended. But other parts of the Punishment are forever. Marilla used to come down to the Qwikpick to hang out with me and Dave, but not only is she not allowed to come to the Qwikpick, according to the Punishment she's not allowed to hang around with me AT ALL!

Why wasn't I allowed to hang out with Marilla but Dave was? Because I live in a trailer park, so I must be a BAD kid. At least that's what her parents think, which is crazy since THEY LIVE IN THE SAME TRAILER PARK! But apparently I'm this really bad influence on Marilla, which is ALSO CRAZY because Marilla is the one who talked me and Dave into both the Poop Fountain trip and the Rat with the Human Face trip.

She wasn't even allowed to talk to me at school and her parents had even asked the principal--who also thinks I'm a bad kid--to make sure she didn't.

All of this was the worst thing possible since I had finally found out that Marilla likes me as more than a friend about ten minutes before the Punishment began. So the Punishment ended up being a terrible punishment for me too, but not as bad as what it was for Marilla, of course.

## SECTION III
## List of Things Dave and I Did to Pass the Time at the Qwikpick Without Marilla

* Got totally sick of playing penny basketball.
* Switched to penny soccer. In my opinion, penny basketball is a game of skill, but penny soccer is a game of skill AND BRAINS! I make sure to tell Dave this every time I beat him, which is almost every time. Why do I win? Because I'm smarter. Right, Dave? Right?
* Wrote about a million different parody versions of "Livin' La Vida Loca"--a song that played on K99 every ten minutes and since the speakers at the Qwikpick play K99 all day, we heard it about 24 x 6 times a day. Pretty soon, you start hearing the "Livin' La Vida Loca" beat in other phrases, like "Going to Drink a Mocha." And you can come up with even more if you add "-a" to the end of a word. Like

this: "Hanging at the Qwik-a Pick-a!"
So we came up with approximately
one million of them! Our best was:
"Eating the Pork-a Rind-a!" Dave
emailed it to Weird Al, but we never
got an answer.

We made these pork-a rind-as for Marilla
since she wasn't there. She said they tasted a
lot better than our singing sounded.

* I had this idea for how to
turn the All-Zombie Marching
Band into a graphic novel,
and--get ready for the shock of
a lifetime--Dave actually liked
my idea. So we spent one whole
weekend plotting it all out, and
if Dave ever gets it drawn, it
will be amazing.

Me and Dave had fun doing that
stuff, but what I really wanted
to be doing was hanging out with
Marilla, and what he really wanted
to be doing was hanging out with
Elizabeth, Marilla's friend who he
likes.
But since neither of those things
was happening, we were just sort
of a Qwikpick Society without any
adventures.

And also a miracle, since Dave has gotten all fussy
about the artwork in it and is taking FOREVER.

## UNOFFICIAL Personal Note

Dave did something really cool for Marilla. Remember how part of her punishment for the Great Rat Disaster was that she had to miss the band's Spring Concert? Every day at school she had to practice the songs even though she knew that she wouldn't get to play them at the concert, and she was really bummed out about it.

So the night of the concert, Dave told his parents he was sick—and actually, he didn't want to lie, so he purposefully ate four Pop-Tarts and drank two V8s so he could truthfully tell his parents he felt sick.

So he missed the concert too.

Back when I thought Dave liked Marilla, I would have thought this was a romantic gesture and I would have been worried about it. But now I realize that Dave is a really good guy and a good friend and I just wish I was in band too, so that I could have done the same thing.

This isn't the weird part—just hold on.

So things went on like that for a while and then one day something weird happened at school.

These three old ladies came in to talk about this local historical site.

So we had an assembly for just the seventh grade in the small assembly room and we listened to these ladies talk . . . or we pretended to.

They handed out these brochures that said "SAVE GREENHILL PLANTATION" and then started telling us why they thought we should save it.

It was some old farmhouse that belonged to this guy named Colonel Shergood a long time ago. You couldn't forget the name because they used it in every sentence.

"Colonel Shergood had the house built for the Shergood family in 1807, and it was originally called Shergood Manor, but in 1822 Colonel Shergood changed . . ." and on and on and on and on and on.

They didn't even have pictures
or anything. You know what they
brought? A chair. They kept talking
about the chair and they said,
"After we're done, you may all look
at Colonel Shergood's chair, but
please do not touch Colonel Shergood's
chair."

Dave whispered, "Trust me, we don't
want to touch the chair, ladies!"

Marilla didn't laugh, but I did
and then I couldn't stop. And that
made Dave start giggling too, which
is pretty rare for Dave.

And for a minute it was really fun
. . . but then Mr. Wayne tapped us on
the shoulder and said, "ISS," which
means In-School Suspension.

As we left the assembly, I was like,
"Yee-ha, we escaped!!!!" And Dave
was like, "Oh no! My life is ruined!
I'm in huge trouble!!!" Dave is the
number-one rule-follower of all time
and doesn't even know what it's like
to get sent to the office.

Here's what it's like: Enter office.

Tell secretary you got sent to ISS. Write
your name on the ISS sheet. Sit. When
bell rings, go to your next class. So . . .
Dave and I were sitting there in the
main office. I was whispering to him to
just relax. Don't worry about it. But of
course he WAS worrying about it.

And then in comes MARILLA!

Now, Marilla getting sent to the
office is just as rare as Dave getting
sent to the office. Dave is the number-
one rule-follower of all time, but
Marilla is the number-one good person
of all time. She just doesn't do the
sort of stuff that gets you sent to the
office.

So Dave and I couldn't believe she
was there. She didn't look like she was
sorry or scared or worried about being
there either. She signed her name
on the sheet like she was signing an
autograph. Then she sat down next to
me.

"Well, I guess I have no choice but
to sit next to Lyle since this is the
only empty seat."

She didn't say this to be mean, but to explain to the secretary why she was sitting next to me when she's not allowed to sit next to me, according to her parents' rules.

I don't think the secretary was aware of those rules because she just looked at Marilla like "Whatever."

Dave and I were dying to know why Marilla was there, but she didn't say anything because the secretary was still vaguely paying attention to us. Then the phone rang and the secretary answered it.

"Marilla," I whispered, "what are you doing here?"

And Marilla said, "I said 'Good'!"

"Why would you get sent to the office for saying 'Good'?"

"Because one of the old ladies said Colonel Shergood's historical house was in jeopardy because they're building a Kmart next to it."

"And you said 'Good'? Do you really like Kmart that much?"

"No, I really hate Colonel Shergood
that much."

Nobody said anything for a minute
because the secretary hung up the
phone.

But then she went back to work and
obviously wasn't paying attention to
us, so then Marilla said, "WE are going
to go and kick him over."

"Who--Shergood? Hasn't he been dead
for like two hundred years?"

"Oh yeah, he's dead, but he's still
standing up . . ." And now Marilla
moved in close and did one of those
whispers that's just barely making
sound waves at all. "And we're going to
go kick his dead *&%!"

The secretary looked up, like she
thought she had heard a bad word,
but when she saw that Marilla had
been talking, she just said, "Shh!
If you want to talk, you can talk to
Mr. Donahue." Obviously, she couldn't
believe that Marilla would say a bad
word in the office.

Me and Dave couldn't believe that

Marilla would say a bad word ANYWHERE! But she said it!

And even though we are bleeping it out of this official report, Marilla says we don't have to. She says that she said what she said and she's not sorry she said it. But Dave says that if we're going to start having bad words in the reports, then he won't help with them anymore, so it's easier just to bleep it out.

Frankly, I think that if anyone ever reads these reports, they're not going to care about whether we bleep out the word "*&%," but they may be a little more concerned about the fact that the whole report is about us breaking into a historic tomb to kick a dead guy in the *&%!!

Before there could be any more cussing or anything else, the bell rang.

"Shoot. Listen, we've got to have a meeting about this. We've gotta make our plan!" Marilla said.

"Uh," said Dave. "There's no need to make a plan, because I'm not doing any of this."

"You're doing it!" said Marilla with her Voice of Authority that she's really good at. "I don't have any more time to explain it now. Here, read the brochure . . ."

And she circled a section of the brochure and handed it to me.

". . . and I'll find some way to meet you tonight at the Qwikpick! Eight o'clock!"

Well, this WAS big. Marilla hasn't been to the Qwikpick in two months because of the Punishment. If she was going to break the Punishment for this, we knew it wasn't a joke.

But we still weren't sure what it was, even after we read the brochure.

# ~ SAVE ~ GREENHILL PLANTATION!

~ Development is encroaching on Greenhill Plantation, the two-hundred-year-old plantation home of Colonel Jezediah Shergood, the Revolutionary War hero. This important historic landmark is in danger of being swallowed up by the planned Gateway Marketplace retail development, which will include a new 80,000-square-foot Kmart, several other stores and restaurants, and four acres of parking lots.

~ While Shergood's home is owned by the Greenhill Preservation Trust, which plans to restore the family mansion so it can be open to the public, the retail development will cover much of the plantation itself. In fact,

Turn page for the circled section.

current plans show an Outback Steakhouse being built less than one hundred yards from the Shergood Family Burial Plot, where, legend has it, Colonel Shergood was buried standing up in his crypt. According to local folklore, the old Southern gentleman asked to be buried in this unusual position so he could continue to keep an eye on his slaves.

~ This is just a small part of Greenhill Plantation's rich historic legacy.

A legacy that is in danger of being lost . . . without your help. Please tell our county commissioners that Greenhill Plantation is not for sale and ask them to vote "No" on the Marketplace rezoning request.

~ And please consider making a donation to the Greenhill Preservation Trust. Together we can protect the past for future generations.

After we read the brochure, Dave said, "Well, it's official. Marilla has gone nuts."

I didn't really know how to argue with him.

# SECTION V
## The Gathering of the Three

Dave hadn't been planning to come to
the Qwikpick that night, but he came
over and we watched Wheel of Fortune
and Jeopardy--which are the only
things you can watch when you only get
channel seven--while we were waiting
for Marilla.

When she still hadn't shown up by
8:00, Dave started to get worried about
getting in trouble, since he's supposed
to be home by 8:30 and it takes about
ten minutes to walk to his house from
the Qwikpick.

But then we heard Marilla stomping
up the steps.

Marilla: Did you read the brochure?
About the slave master being buried
standing up.

Anytime you see a conversation in the official report,
it may not be the exact words everybody said. I try to
take notes and then write it all up afterward, but it's
hard, because people talk faster than I can write.

Dave: Yeah and it seems really unlikely. I mean, how could--

Marilla: Unlikely?? How about INHUMAN? This awful @#&%*$% had a farm full of slaves and when he died--

Lyle (me): Marilla, what is with you and the cussing? I never heard you say a bad word ever!

*Dave was too appalled to speak.*

Marilla: Well, (a) I am tired of being a good little girl, especially when I get treated like a convicted criminal, and (b) this guy really was an @#&%*$%! I mean, first of all, he was a slave driver who had this big fancy house and a big plantation and the only "work" he did for it was hassling his slaves. So then he finally dies with a smug smile on his face because he believes that he was their master and will continue to be their master forever and ever because he is still watching over them! And now, all these years later, he's still smug! Because instead of people being like "That guy was an @#&%*$%," these ladies are like "Oh, Let's save Shergood's house" and "Isn't it cool how he had himself buried standing up?"

Dave: I don't think any of those old ladies ever say things are "cool."

Marilla: You know what I mean! They've made HIM the local legend, the folk hero of this story. NO! UH-UH! This @#&%*$% is the VILLAIN, and if I want to call him an @#&%*$%, I'll call him an @#&%*$%.

Dave: You've got a point, but couldn't we just call him a big fat jerk instead?

Lyle: Actually, that's offensive to overweight people.

I don't like people using "fat" as an insult because my mom is pretty overweight and upset about being overweight, and every time somebody says it, I know it makes her feel bad.

Dave: Well, call him something that's not a bad word or I'm done.

Lyle: Dave, no one is making you say a bad word. You're not breaking a rule!

Dave: I still don't like it. Just call him something else. How about Colonel Goofpooper?

Marilla: Look, you two can argue about what to call him all the way there and all the way back, but can I finish my ding-dang sentence?

*See, I told you Marilla is in charge.*

Marilla: Okay, my point is, this guy died a "winner" and people still treat him like a "winner" and he's really an evil son of a--uh, potato--

Lyle: Son of a potato?

Marilla: You know what I mean, Lyle. I'm trying to keep Dave from getting hung up on what we call him! Anyway, it's about two hundred years late, but I think we should go knock him down.

Lyle: Oh! Like some kind of cosmic justice!

Marilla: Right! I mean, maybe that's why God put us together. Our first two adventures were just warm-ups. Now we have a mission to do something that really needs to get done . . . That's why I feel like it's okay for us to break a few earthly rules . . . Because we are going to deliver justice for this guy breaking God's rules.

Dave: Uh, yeah. That's my main point. What about YOU breaking God's rules? You're talking about some serious commandment-violating! You're already telling lies to come here tonight--

Marilla: Actually, I told them I need to get some leaves for biology class. So I need to find some fast on the way back.

Dave: Right, a few dead leaves will totally explain why you just broke every rule they made about not coming to the Qwikpick and not seeing Lyle and--

Marilla: I know it's not being completely honest, but this is important.

Dave: You're the one who's always going on about the Ten Commandments. This is going to be a serious heavy-duty violation of number four: honoring your mother and father.

Marilla: Look, Dave, I've been honoring my mother and stepfather by putting up with these stupid new rules of theirs and staying out of the Qwikpick and missing the Spring Concert and not talking to Lyle at school--and I really miss talking to you, Lyle. I've honored them plenty. So now I'm going to honor my father--my REAL father--by kicking down one of the slave masters who used to rule over our ancestors.

Lyle: Your real father?

Marilla: Yeah. Dale's my stepfather, you know.

Lyle: Oh, so is your real father . . . uh . . . is he a . . . uh . . . African American?

Marilla: Yeah, he's black. You didn't know that?

Lyle: No, you never told me.

Dave: Me neither.

Marilla: Oh . . . I figured you guys had seen him. He used to come by every couple of months to pick me up and take me out shopping and stuff. ANYWAY, I'm going to kick over this corpse in his honor and my grandmother's and all the rest of his part of the family all the way back to when we were slaves.

Lyle: That's pretty cool!

Marilla: Yeah, I can be like HYAHHHH, now you can go to--

Dave: Don't say it! Say potato!

Marilla: Actually, I wasn't going to say
. . . H-E-L-L. I was going to say Gehenna.
That's where REALLY bad people go. Think
about it. This guy was an actual slave
master. He thought he owned people and
that they had to work for him and that
it was okay to whip them if they didn't.
Dude, my great-great-great-grandmother
could have been one of his slaves.

Dave: Whaaaaat?

*Very skeptically in that way that he has that drives you crazy.*

Marilla: Right, my grandmother--my
dad's mother, Nana Georgie--told me her
great-grandmother was a slave. Probably
not on that farm, but somewhere around
here. I'm not ashamed to say that. I'm
proud of her. She survived all that
evil. It's SHERGOOD's great-great-great-
grandchildren who should be ashamed!

Dave: I get it. But what does kicking him
do?

Marilla: Well, first of all he deserves
to be kicked, and second it ENDS this

*$%#--I'm sorry, Dave, but that's the only word for it--about him watching over "his" slaves forever, and third, what if one day I meet my great-great-great-grandmother in heaven? Then I can tell her, "I kicked over a slave master for you."

Dave: Okay, those are all awesome . . . for you. I'm still not sure why I need to go.

Marilla: Dave, this adventure is perfect for you too.

Dave: Uh, how?

Marilla: Well, first of all, you don't have to be black to know that slave masters were totally evil and deserve to be kicked over. But also because you are waaaaay overdue for breaking a rule. You NEED to break a rule. And this is the time to start . . . when you know that you are being just a little bit bad but your purpose is to do something really, really good.

Dave: (thinking)

Marilla: So anyway . . . I've got to go before I get re-grounded. You guys figure out the maps and details and stuff. Then we'll go TCB!

Lyle and Dave: TCB?

Marilla: Take care of business!

She shouted this as she was running down the stairs.

"Oh, potato!" said Dave, looking at his watch. "I'm going to have to mooove it, mooove it to get home by eight thirty!" And he took off too.

I got out some paper and starting writing down that conversation as best as I could remember it. Because even though we hadn't all officially agreed that we were going, I knew we were going and that we'd need an official report about it.

UNOFFICIAL Personal Note

Okay, dispensing cosmic justice and kicking over this dead slave master sounds pretty good.

But this isn't exactly what I was hoping for. See, you may remember that on the last QAS adventure there was a tiny bit of romance at the end, when I finally found out for sure that Marilla likes me. And since then there's been NO chance for us to even talk about what happened. So I hoped if we got to go on an adventure there'd be a chance for . . . you know. But kicking dead bodies and romance don't really go together.

Then again, poop and rats and romance don't really go together either, so who knows!

## Section V Addendum
## Why Dave Is Ready to Break
## a Rule

You may be wondering about what
Marilla meant when she said that Dave
needed to break a rule.

Well, it's a sad and painful story
and it all starts with the fact that
Dave is

The Number-One Rule-Follower of All
Time.

Being the number-one rule-follower of
all time can really stink and I think
Dave was getting tired of it, especially
after the A Bad Bee incident.

Here's what happened.

When I was banned from hanging out
with Marilla, it meant I couldn't eat
lunch with her and Dave at the nerd
table anymore. It was Marilla letting
me sit with them that made us all
friends in the first place! And now I
had to find somewhere else to go.

There was one good thing about this: Jeremy, who eats at the far end of the nerd table, is the worst person in the world and for some reason is always giving me a hard time. So at least I wouldn't have to put up with him anymore.

But this was balanced out by another really bad thing, because the only seat I could find was next to ... Carrie Felman, this girl who's like a female Jeremy.

So I thought that was going to be my life forever, but it only lasted about a week. Because soon Dave was at my table too, and all because he is the number-one rule-follower of all time.

Here's what happened. In language arts we had to read this book called <u>Tom Sawyer Abroad</u>.

NOT <u>Tom Sawyer</u> ... <u>Tom Sawyer ABROAD</u>. We were supposed to read like forty pages a night.

I would try to make myself read it ... and I just couldn't. I would force

myself to read and I would hit a chapter
like "Tom Respects The Flea," which is
actually about Tom respecting fleas, and
I just couldn't get through it. So I fell
way behind, and the night before the
test I would have had to read like 150
pages to catch up.

# Tom Sawyer Abroad
## Mark Twain

*In case you don't believe me!*

## Table of Contents

I asked my mom what to do about the test and she told me that stuff like that happens in real life and you just have to do the best you can. Since I didn't have time to read it all, maybe I should try to skim it all, she said.

Even that was hard, but I tried.

So the next day I got a C- on the test. Not that bad really, since I usually get about that even when I've read a book because Ms. Van Metre uses these multiple-choice tests she gets from some teacher's guide that only have five questions. Since there are only five questions, if you get one wrong: B-. Get two wrong: C-.

And then the next day Ms. Van Metre announced that we were going to have to take a new test on the book because she had "been alerted to" a major cheating scandal: A student who she would not name had explained to her that many students had known the answers to the test ahead of time.

Oh no, I thought . . . DAVE!

And I was right. It was Dave. Not one of the ones who was cheating, of course.

As previously stated, Dave is the number-one rule-follower of all time. He would never cheat!

But if there is any kid at school who would do something insane like tell a teacher about something like this, it's Dave.

"I had to do it, Lyle," he told me that night at the Qwikpick. "If people want to cheat, that's their problem, not mine. But Jeremy told EVERYBODY at the lunch table that the answers were a bad bee."

"A bad bee?"

"Right. A, B, A, D, B. Someone who had Van Metre first period started telling people in other classes that those were the answers and it spread around. EVERYBODY in class knew."

"I didn't know."

"That's because you eat lunch over there in reject-land."

"True," I said. "But back to the subject, I thought you said you didn't care if other people cheated."

"I don't."

"Then why did you tell Van Metre?"

"Because once I had heard 'a bad b,' I was part of the cheating too."

"But, Dave, you actually read the stupid book. You could have just answered the questions."

"But I already knew the answers! That's cheating."

"Not if you knew the answers from reading the book!"

"But how could I know I knew the answers when I already knew the answers?"

So I can't really explain Dave to you. The thing is, he DID tell Van Metre. He didn't tell her any names of any cheaters, but he told her. She made us retake the test and a lot of kids who had gotten an A+ ended up with a C- or worse. (Because almost no one was able to read the whole book!)

End result: Everyone (except me and Marilla) now hates Dave. (I wasn't even particularly mad at him since somehow I got a B- on the retest!)

Jeremy was really obnoxious about it, of course, but the worst part for

Dave was that Elizabeth was really mad about it too.

Basically, Dave likes Elizabeth the way I like Marilla. But here's the thing. Even though Marilla isn't allowed to hang around with me, I know she wants to and that's nice. Things aren't so nice for Dave. Elizabeth is ALLOWED to hang out with him, she just doesn't want to. And even though they're in band together, they are not "band buddies" like a lot of band people are.

So Dave already had problems with Elizabeth, and this test thing just added to them, big-time. Elizabeth has Van Metre for first period and took the test without cheating. Then when she had to take it again, she got a worse grade. And she's one of those people who are really fussy about their grades. And then, just to make it a complete disaster, Dave refused to apologize to her or anybody else about it. So he had to abandon the nerd table and join me (and Carrie Felman) at the reject table. (The empty seat was actually on the

44

other side of Carrie, but she agreed
to move so we could sit together. Not
to be nice. Just so she didn't have to
sit between us.)

So here's the weird thing. I ended
up at the reject table for being "bad"
and Dave ended up there for being
"good." Anyway, that's why the last two
months haven't been as bad for me as I
expected, but they've been a lot worse
for Dave than he expected. And it's
why Dave was ready to stop being the
number-one rule-follower of all time
and actually break a rule.

# SECTION VI
## Plans

"Marilla has gone insane," said Dave at our first planning session.

"She's not insane."

"She wants to kick a dead person. That's the definition of insane."

He said he wished Marilla could come to our planning sessions so that he could talk her out of it. And I told him if he tried that, she would just get mad and call him a wimp and talk him back into it. So we had to just keep on meeting and planning. ↖

Dave did try to talk her out of it at school, but she would always say, "Are you crazy? We can't talk about this at school. Do you want to get caught or something?" And of course Dave doesn't ever want to get caught, so he never got to talk to her about it.

↑

There's no real reason why this can't be in the official report, it's just that I forgot to mention it when I was typing. If I ever get the computer working, I'll be able to just go back and insert this kind of thing.

So Dave and I spent a lot of time looking at maps, trying to figure out how we were going to get all the way over there to the far side of Crickenburg where the plantation is.

Dave had one of his mom's real estate maps that shows every little road and alley and everything. If you were riding a bike, you'd just take South Franklin Street over to 24 and then ride out 24 for a few miles. But as we've mentioned in the official reports before, you can't ride your bike on South Franklin Street. The traffic there is nuts because everyone is going to Wal-Mart (and a few are going to the Qwikpick, of course).

There was actually a pretty good route we found that would have gone parallel to South Franklin Street, but the road ends in a dead end and then you have to run across some railroad tracks and go through some woods and you come out behind the new Kroger.

But Dave was like, "No way. We're breaking too many rules already without illegally crossing the railroad tracks. Not only is it against the law, but it's also dangerous and . . ." etc., etc.

He had a point. My dad had a friend in high school who was goofing around on the tracks and got killed. Or at least that's what my dad says.

So we were pretty much stuck taking South Franklin Street (which has a bridge over the tracks), but we would have to walk it, which was going to be a LONG walk.

The other parts of our planning involved rounding up flashlights and tools. Dave says that every account of breaking into a crypt ever says the people use a crowbar. So we had to find a crowbar. Maybe in ye olden days people had crowbars lying around everywhere, but we couldn't find one. Since my family lives in a trailer, we don't have like a big garage full of tools and stuff. And Dave says his mom doesn't believe in do-it-yourself home repairs because it lessens the value of a house. So they don't have a bunch of tools either.

"Maybe we should go buy one at Wal-Mart," I said.

"First of all," said Dave, "I really doubt Wal-Mart has crowbars. Second of all, we don't want to leave a paper trail."

"First of all," I said, "Wal-Mart has everything. Second of all . . . a what?"

"A paper trail . . . like if a detective were to investigate this, the first thing he'd do is find out who had bought crowbars recently. Wal-Mart has records of all that stuff."

"Do you really think a detective is going to investigate this?"

"I sure hope not. Frankly, I hope this doesn't happen at all. But Marilla told us to plan, and so my job is to plan as well as I can. So I say no paper trail."

"Then where are we going to get a crowbar?"

"Actually, maybe we should just forget the crowbar. Then when we actually get down there, we won't be able to open the door and Marilla will have to give up and we can go home without desecrating a grave."

"Desecrating?"

"Yes, that's the verb form of what Marilla wants to do. She wants to desecrate. As for me, I do not want to desecrate. I want to buy an old Beatles album at the record shop."

"Yes, I've heard you say that one hundred times."

"And I'll say it one hundred more times! I'll say it one thousand times. I'll say it--"

ET CETERA.

Then I found a crowbar in the supply room at the Qwikpick, so I guess a lot of that conversation was really pointless.

## Section VII
## Dave Chickens Out

Memorial Day is always on Monday, right?

Well, the Saturday before Memorial Day, Dave calls me up and says he's not going to do it.

"Is this because you went to church today?" I asked him.

"It's a synagogue and yes."

"Well, YOU are going to have to tell Marilla, because I'm not even allowed to talk to her."

So he calls her. Then he calls me back. "She's calling an emergency meeting at the Dumpster behind the Qwikpick at eight thirty," he said.

So we both got there at 8:30 and then a couple of minutes later Marilla comes racing down the hill on her bike and skids to a stop at the Dumpster.

"What's the deal, wimps?"

"I'm not the wimp!" I said.

"I'm not either," said Dave, "but I have analyzed this from—"

"I don't have time for a speech, Dave. What's the problem?"

"Okay . . . I would do it," he said, "but if we get caught and arrested for vandalizing a historic property and the judge asked us why we did it, 'cosmic justice' isn't going to cut the mustard."

"Cut the mustard?" I said.

"It's a saying! It means we could seriously end up not just in trouble but in jail. And I am not just saying this because I always follow the rules. I am ready to break a rule. But I am not ready to go to jail."

"So," said Marilla, "what you're saying—if we scrape off the mustard—is that you're up for this adventure, but only if we can lessen the risk of getting caught?"

"ELIMINATE the risk!"

"Fine," said Marilla. "Lyle, you figure out how to eliminate the risk. I gotta go! See you Monday morning."

And she rode off.

We just sort of stood there like
idiots and watched her go.

"You got it figured out yet?" asked
Dave about thirty seconds later.

"Actually, yes," I said, and, yes,
I was kind of smug about it, because
it's not that often I figure out
something before Dave. And somehow
during those thirty seconds the whole
plan came to me.

# SECTION VIII
## Lyle Saves the Day

I asked Dave if it was too braggy to call this section "Lyle Saves the Day" and he said yes . . .

Why am I naming it "Lyle Saves the Day"? Because I saved the day!

Here's the plan I came up with that changed everything.

Fact: Memorial Day is one of the days we have off from school, and days off from school are good days for a Qwikpick adventure, because our parents are busy and are just glad that we're old enough that they don't have to make special arrangements for us anymore.

Even when we were younger, I got to hang around the Qwikpick on days off, but up until a year ago Dave got dropped off at Rainbow Rangers Day Care and would have to spend all day there playing Hi, Ho, Cherry-O with preschoolers.

54

Fact: On Memorial Day, people get plastic flower wreaths and put them in front of soldiers' graves and statues.

Fact: These wreaths cost $12.99 at Wal-Mart.

Fact: Colonel Jezediah Shergood was a soldier in the Revolutionary War, according to the brochure from the Greenhill ladies.

The plan: We buy one of those wreaths and carry it to Greenhill Plantation. If anything goes wrong and someone catches us near the tomb, we tell them that we're just there to honor Col. Jezediah Shergood, and we put down the wreath and Dave plays taps on his bugle. It's the perfect camouflage!! Now there is simply no way to get in trouble. If anyone comes anywhere near us, we switch from corpse-kickers to model citizens.

Dave's concern: First of all, I play the trumpet, not the bugle. Second of all, what do we do when they ask why three model citizens are carrying a crowbar?

Lyle's answer: I've been thinking about that. I think the crowbar is too much. We shouldn't use a crowbar. That crosses the line between an adventure and vandalism. If we can't get at Shergood and knock him down without using a crowbar to bust the tomb open, then we're just going to have to let him be for now.

Dave's verdict: I can live with this plan.

Marilla's response: Lyle, awesome plan! You saved the day! One thing: I think when it's over, we need to find a good place to put the wreath and actually honor soldiers with it. Otherwise, it's pretty disrespectful.

However, either way, Dave should not play taps. That would not honor ANYONE!

Marilla's response also included a hug! Not a half-hug but a real hug! Things have come a long way since the poop fountain!

## SECTION IX
## Sunday: Pre-Memorial Day
## Preparations

1. Lyle and Dave go to Wal-Mart and buy a nice wreath of red, white, and blue plastic flowers.

2. Marilla gets permission to sleep over at Elizabeth's; her parents are going to pick her up there the next day (Monday--Memorial Day) at 4 p.m.

3. Dave gets temporarily excited because he thinks maybe Elizabeth will come on this adventure, but I have to break it to him that she won't. She's just going to sit around her house watching talk shows all day instead! But he's still hoping that when we stop at her house she'll decide to come.

Dave, you need to find somebody more interesting to be in love with!

4. Finalize route: Lyle and Dave will
   ride their bikes to Elizabeth's
   house (1.5 miles). Then Lyle, Dave,
   and Marilla will walk across town
   to the plantation site (3 miles).
   We'll TCB. Then walk back to
   Elizabeth's on slightly different
   route to leave wreath at county
   courthouse soldier statue (3.5
   miles). Total walking: 6.5 miles!!!
   Plus 3 miles of bike riding total
   for Dave and me! YIKES! AND we
   absolutely positively no question
   need to be back at Elizabeth's by
   3 p.m., just in case Marilla's
   parents come by early.

5. Pack snacks, but no lunch because
   Marilla says the route should take
   us near her favorite restaurant.
   But she won't tell us which one it
   is.

## SECTION X
## The Qwikpick

So Memorial Day finally came and step one was for me to get to Dave's house on my bike.

By the time I got up, both my parents were already working down at the Qwikpick. (I wasn't supposed to get to Dave's house until 9:30, to give his mom time to leave for work, so I headed to the Qwikpick first to get our snacks.)

UNOFFICIAL personal note

No one believes this, but there are some great advantages to living in a trailer park, especially Crab Creek Estates. It's a great place for bike riding, especially when you are going to the Qwikpick, since it's downhill all the way. You can actually coast the entire way from our house to the Qwikpick parking lot.

It took me about 150 tries before I finally did it without pedaling once, but now I can do it just about every time unless something slows me down. This time there were a lot of worms stretched out in the road and I like to dodge them, if possible, so it was not a perfect coast. Also, I had to dodge Jennifer from the Green Trailer (most of the Crab Creek Estates trailers are brown, but hers is green, which is how she got her name), who was walking back up the hill with a plastic bag from the Qwikpick.

And she was smoking, of course. That was probably the real reason she had gone down there, to get cigarettes. My dad says that one of the worst things about working at a convenience store is selling stuff to people when you know they can't afford it and shouldn't be buying it anyway. (Of course, both of my parents smoke too, so it's kind of unfair of him to say that about other people, although Jennifer really CAN'T afford it since she doesn't have a job.)

"Yo, Lyle, baby!"

"Hi, Jennifer!"

"Got a date?"

"Sorta."

"Woowoowoo!"

This is basically the same conversation I always have with Jennifer. When I say I don't have a date, she always says, "I'm available, hawney." This is just a joke, because she is about my parents' age.

Not only are most of the people who live here nice, but for some reason most of them talk to you like you're an adult too. I mean, when you all live this close to each other, you run into each other all the time. And most of the adults here say stuff like "Yo, Lyle" or "Hey, what's up, dude" as if we're friends. There's nobody here who says normal grown-up stuff like, "Well, young man, are you excited about summer vacation?" If they wanted to know about your summer vacation, they'd say, "You guys going to the beach?"

I dropped my bike next to the Dumpster and went in the back door. My dad was busy with a line of customers, but my mother was in the "DrinkZone" helping Larry set up the new flavored-coffee machine. Larry has been complaining about this new machine for about a month. He says it doesn't really make coffee, just squirts out goop for people who want dessert for breakfast. But the Qwikpick corporate offices told him he had to have one because they're big moneymakers.

"It's finally here," I said.

"Yeah and it doesn't work!" said Larry. Sometimes Larry is in a great mood for joking around. And sometimes he can be scary.

This was Scary Larry. (Marilla got the points for that Rhyme-jitsu a long time ago.) He had one arm way up inside the machine and thick goop was dripping all over him.

Mom and I retreated to a safe distance.

"Hey, Mom. I'm going over to Dave's."

"Yeah . . . and THEN what are you doing?"

My mother was onto us! I'm not exactly sure how, but she clearly knew we had some sort of plan. "We're going across town to . . . mess around."

"Uh-huh. Okay. Listen, watch the cars."

"Okay."

"I'm serious. I worry more about you getting hit than getting into trouble."

"I--"

"I mean, tracking mud into a hotel is one thing, but getting hit by a Buick is another."

I don't know if people even drive Buicks anymore. I don't think I've ever seen one. But whenever my mother talks about getting hit by a car, it's always a Buick.

"We're doing double doubles today, so stop back by."

That sentence probably doesn't make any sense to you. She means

The good news about a "double double" is that my parents should both have tomorrow off together—they'll sleep in while I go to school and then, because they made extra money, we'll probably go out to eat for supper. The day after a "double double" is usually a fun one for us.

that she and my Dad are both working double shifts because of the holiday traffic, so they'll still be working when I get back.

But the important thing here is that my mom was giving me permission to have a little adventure. Marilla and Dave were both having to be sneaky about getting out of the house, but my parents are a lot better about letting me do stuff. I didn't want to explain to her about kicking over the corpse and everything, but I think that even if I had she wouldn't have stopped me.

"Bye, honey," said my mom, and "Bye, dude," said my dad.

And I was off!

# SECTION XI
## Dave's House

Dave has a different way of dealing with his mother: stay in bed until she leaves for work and then write a note. Today's note said: "I went to Elizabeth's. Back for supper. Dave."

Dave says this note is better than a haiku. He says it has a thousand meanings in just eight words. "First of all, it's the truth. We ARE going to Elizabeth's. True, we're also going to a plantation to desecrate a grave, but I didn't lie about that. I just didn't mention it.

"Secondly, dropping the name of a girl. My notes usually say, 'Gone to Lyle's,' but I couldn't write that today because that wouldn't have been true. So whatever I write will be out of the ordinary and could cause increased interest . . .

"However, when my mother sees Elizabeth's name, she will be interested in the wrong thing. She's so desperate for me to have a girlfriend that tonight she will be trying to figure out if there was any kissing without actually asking about kissing. Of course, you and I know that the chances of me and Elizabeth doing any kissing are zero in a million, but my mother never gives up hope."

*Dave hasn't given up hope yet either, but he won't admit it.*

"So she's going to ask a bunch of questions like 'How are things between you and Elizabeth?' and 'Have you thought about inviting Elizabeth to go to the pool with us next Saturday?'"

"ARE you going to ask Elizabeth to go to the pool with you?" I asked.

"Of course not! The last thing in the world I need is for Elizabeth to see me with my shirt off . . . not that she would actually go anywhere with me anyway."

*He's right. She wouldn't.*

"But my point is that having the whole Elizabeth discussion for the hundredth time will have completely distracted my mother from asking where we did go.

"Speaking of which, let's go . . . I think I hear my evil brothers stirring upstairs."

# SECTION XII
## Elizabeth

So we rode our bikes over to
Elizabeth's. It was a little hard to ride
while carrying a shopping bag with the
big plastic Wal-Mart wreath in it . . .
but not enough to make me crash or
anything.

We got to Elizabeth's and she and
Marilla were out on the porch waiting
for us.

I'm sure Dave had something planned
that he was going to say to Elizabeth to
try and talk her into coming with us,
but she started talking first.

"Who you gonna call?" she yelled when
we were still half a block away.

Dave fell for it. He was just happy
she was talking to him.

"Huh?"

"Ghostbusters!" Elizabeth yelled. "Uh
. . . Lyle and Dave ain't afraid of no
ghost! Doo doo doo doo! Ghostbusters!"

And she started doing a little
dance, which I really doubt anybody

*It's pretty clear that Dave doesn't actually read the official reports, so I think I'm safe to stick this in. I'm sure he would say that he NEVER flirts with Elizabeth, but in fact that's ALL he ever does.*

in Ghostbusters ever did, although I haven't seen the movie, since it isn't part of the Qwikpick break room collection.

"Okay, let's go," said Marilla and she started walking away. But of course Dave wanted to linger and flirt with Elizabeth.

"Are you a Ghostbusters fan? Me too. I LOVE that movie," said Dave.

"I'm not talking about the movie!" said Elizabeth. (And just a reminder that anytime this report says that someone said something, it may not be an exact quote, it's just how I remember it.) "I'm talking about you guys!"

"What are you--"

"Marilla told me all about what you guys are going to do and--"

"Lyle and Dave . . . let's GO!" said Marilla.

It looked like she had not really enjoyed the sleepover with Elizabeth.

"—and I asked her if she was afraid that the slave master's ghost was going to start haunting you guys after you wake him up by entering his tomb!"

"CAN WE JUST GO?" snarled Marilla.

"And she said she's not afraid of ghosts!" finished Elizabeth. "So you guys are like the Ghostbusters! Doo doo doo doo doo . . . Who you gonna call?"

Elizabeth seemed to think this was hilarious. I sure didn't. And, obviously, Marilla was tired of hearing it. Even Dave couldn't quite force himself to laugh at it.

I leaned my bike against the side of the porch and started walking after Marilla, but Dave sort of hung behind.

"Are you going to come too?" he asked.

Marilla groaned. "Dave! Let's move it out!" she yelled. Then she whispered, "If she comes, I'm going to lose my brain."

Luckily for Marilla's brain, Elizabeth had no interest in coming along.

But she did have more to say about

the ghost. "No way! I wouldn't go for a million bucks! I'm afraid of the Curse of the Slave Master's Tomb! Aren't you afraid of the Curse of the Slave Master's Tomb, Dave?"

"Uh, I don't think there's a curse."

"Of course there's a curse! Haven't you--"

And she had a lot more to say about it. Dave was in heaven. This was the most Elizabeth had ever talked to him. But she wasn't REALLY talking to him. She was doing that thing people do sometimes, when Person A and Person B have some kind of private joke, so Person A has a fake conversation with Person C so that Person B can hear.

But in this case Person B didn't want to hear any more because she was sick and tired of the private joke.

"DAVE!" Marilla yelled.

"Dude, come on!" I said.

Somehow I seem to get caught up in more of those kinds of conversations than real ones at school.

"Listen, Dave," said Elizabeth, "why do you want to spend a day off from school walking all the way across town to get in trouble AND stir up an angry ghost? I told Marilla we could all just hang out at my house today and watch movies and stuff."

"That sounds--" started Dave, but then Marilla started yelling at Elizabeth.

"You're driving me crazy! Will you give it a REST!"

"This is my house! I'll say anything I want to say. I'll sing anything I want to sing. If you don't like it, you can leave!"

Then she stomped into her house, yelled "Ghostbusters!" one more time, and slammed the door.

Marilla stomped out of the yard and started down the sidewalk.

Dave looked like he wanted to knock on Elizabeth's door.

"Let's just go," I said, and we ran to catch up with Marilla.

## SECTION XIII
## Attack of the Weirdo
## Hoodlums (Us)

Well, here we were . . . for the first time in a long, long time, I was with Marilla and we could talk to each other and have fun just like the old days.

But Marilla was way too mad to have fun.

"Arrrgh!" she yelled. And it's weird when someone yells in a quiet little neighborhood like where Elizabeth lives. I imagined a bunch of old people peeking out their windows to see what all the yelling was about. They probably thought we were a bunch of hoodlums.

"Marilla," I said when I finally caught up to her. (She was walking FAST.) "What just happened back there? Why were you so mad about Elizabeth singing 'Ghostbusters'?"

Actually, since we were going to kick over a corpse, I guess they were right.

*Marilla is about to recite an entire conversation, so I'm going to break it up into pieces so hopefully it will make more sense.*

Marilla stopped so quickly, me and Dave almost ran into her. She whirled around and sort of half yelled: "Because she has been singing it since nine thirty last night!"

"Did you guys watch the movie or something?" asked Dave.

"No, it's got nothing to do with the movie . . . UG . . . She was TRYING to drive me crazy. Okay, see, it was like this.

She wanted me to stay at her house all day, even though I had already told her I was going to do something with you guys.

So she's like, "What's so important?"

So I told her.

And she said it was the dumbest thing she'd ever heard.

And so I told her that's why we didn't invite her. Because we knew she would say that.

And she said she'd said it because it was one hundred percent true.

And then she tried to talk me out of it. She said if we picked something else, then she would join us."

"That sounds--" started Dave, but Marilla kept going.

"And I said no, we wouldn't pick something else, because this is important.
And she was like, "Whooo, yeah, it's SO important. You guys have to go kick a guy who's been dead for centuries. You're like the Ghostbusters."
And then whenever I tried to say something she'd go, "You ain't afraid of no ghost."
And it was about the biggest fight we ever had and normally I would have called my parents to come get me, but if I did that, then it would have messed up our plans for today. So we both went to bed really mad. And this morning I tried to explain it to her again, but she just started back with the Ghostbusters thing. And then we

74

had to pretend we weren't fighting in front of her mom. But once her mom left, we had a really big fight. And then you guys showed up.

The end."

"That's not the end," said Dave. "The end is, we all need to go back so you can apologize to Elizabeth and we can be friends again."

"WHAT?? Why should I apologize!?!"

"Because you hurt her feelings! You were basically saying that you didn't want her to hang around with us."

"No, I wasn't!"

"Yeah, she was trying to change the plans so she could be part of it too and you shut her out."

"You just want us to go back there so you can sit around her house all day flirting with her."

"I DON'T FLIRT!" Dave yelled.

And now I was sure the old people were calling the police to say we were not just hoodlums but actual weirdo hoodlums.

"Well, you can go back if you want!" snarled Marilla. "I'm leaving!"

And she turned around and started walking again.

"You're going the wrong way," said Dave with his sneeriest voice.

"Look, Buttpain . . . ," she snarled. ". . . give us the map and you can go back to Elizabeth and you can both--"

So this whole time I was standing there trying to figure out how to save this situation.

And then I remembered: "The Musical!"

I know I used the world "snarled" a second ago, but this was a snarlier snarl. And can you believe she called Dave "Buttpain"?

And I admit, part of me was wondering if I SHOULD save the situation . . . I mean, if Dave went back to Elizabeth, then I'd have all day with Marilla. But if he did, then this wouldn't be an official Qwikpick Adventure Society adventure anymore.

# SECTION XIV
## "The Musical!"

"The Musical!" is a game we came up with one night at the Qwikpick.

We had just tried to watch one of the old videotapes. These videotapes are what's left over from when the Qwikpick rented videos. Basically, anything that anyone had interest in watching was sold, so what was left was weird and lousy.

We had watched all the ones that sounded at least remotely interesting--and a couple of them had been good!--so at this particular point we were down to watching the ones that didn't sound even remotely interesting.

This movie was called Gypsy River. And it was so incredibly bad. It was not about gypsies OR rivers!

It was about a guy named Tony with a pet monkey. But it wasn't really a comedy . . . at least it wasn't very

And of course this was back when Marilla was still allowed to hang out with us.

funny, because the guy was all
depressed and he and the monkey kept
getting drunk and people would yell
at them. And to make it even worse,
whenever they showed a close-up of the
monkey, they had obviously switched
to a puppet. And the puppet monkey
would waggle its eyebrows.

So after about ten minutes we were
groaning and complaining and ready
to turn it off, but then there was
this scene in a grocery store. The
guy is buying a six-pack of beer, and
the store manager runs up and says,
"Your monkey ate six dollars' worth of
asparagus!" After that, the guy and
the monkey run out of the store with
the beer and the manager calls the
cops and blah blah blah . . .

But we weren't paying attention
anymore because we were all saying,
"Excuse me, sir, your monkey ate
six dollars' worth of asparagus" in
different accents and stuff. And it
got funnier and funnier.

And then Marilla goes, "Gypsy River:

The Musical!" And then she sings, "Your monkey ate six dollars' worth of as-par-uuhuhhhhhuuhhhhhuuhhhhhhuuhhhhhuh-hhhhhhhhhhhh . . ." and her voice was getting higher and higher and then she waves her hands like a conductor and Dave and I know that we're supposed to join in and we all went, "GUS!"

That may not seem funny now, but it sure seemed funny then. It was the only time that Larry ever came up to the break room to tell us to quiet down.

And when we performed the line for him, he said, "Okay, I can see why you busted a gut over that. Go right ahead."

And right after he left, Dave said, "Busted a gut?"

And Marilla added, "The Musical!"

So that is when we started adding "The Musical!" anytime somebody said something weird.

A classic example: In the lunch line, Liam Quesenberry asked for tater tots AND tater wedges, and Paula the lunch lady goes, "You can't get tots AND wedges!"

"Tots and Wedges: The Musical!"

"Hey, dumb kid, don't you know
You may only eat one type o' potato . . ."

When Dave sang that at the lunch table,
Jeremy said we were embarrassing him
and he'd move if we didn't stop. So the
whole rest of the table got up and sang it
together! (But he didn't move.)

Other favorite "The Musical!"s:

Your favorite infomercial is now your
favorite Broadway smash:
"I Was Very Impressed with the
Shamwow: The Musical"

Animal fun for the kiddies:
"Positive Ducks: The Musical"

A toe-tapping musical revue:
"Actually, It's in Wisconsin: The
Musical"

Animal fun for the kiddies, with a
heartbreaking ending you'll never
forget:

"Two Groundhogs and a Dead Skunk: The
Musical"

A touching family drama:
"My Brothers Tried to Wipe Their Toe Jam
on Me: The Musical" .

A touching family drama set at Wal-Mart.
"Noah, I'm Going to Put the Toy Back and
We're Leaving if You Don't Stop. I Mean
It! You're Not Being Very Mature! Okay,
I'm Putting the Toy Back! You Don't Want
Me to Put the Toy Back, Do You?: The
Musical."

And its sequel:
"I Can't Believe Noah Got the Toy!: The
Musical!"

   You can try this yourself. Anytime
somebody says something odd and there's a
weird little silence after it, just repeat
what they said and add "The Musical!" Then
just sort of sing it and see if you can
think of something to rhyme with it. (Being
a Rhyme-jitsu master helps.)

# SECTION XV
## I Sing

I usually just sort of chant-talk
the words when I do a "The Musical!"
but I felt like I needed to really
sing this time or they would ignore
me or not even hear me. So I sort of
sing-shouted:

"Buttpain! Won't you come with us,
Buttpain?
We've got a long way to go . . .
To kick a dead guy with our toe.
So won't you come with us, dear . . .
BUTTPAIN???"

"EXCUSE ME!" Someone was shouting
at us!
"EXCUSE ME! You children need
to go somewhere else! You have been
standing in front of my house for ten
minutes and you've been noisy and
very disrespectful of people trying to
enjoy a day off."
It was a really annoying lady with

what my dad calls a "hair helmet" and
lots of makeup on sticking her head
out of her front door. So all we could
see was her head yelling at us. She was
really getting worked up.

"And now you've started yelling about
butts? Excuse me?"

Dave was terrified, and I was super-
embarrassed, but Marilla snorted.

"Oh, you think it's funny?" said the
woman. "Well, I think you need to be
mindful of--"

"Let's go," said Marilla.

The woman kept yakking at us as we
walked away.

"Great, Lyle. Now you got us in
trouble. Thanks!" said Dave.

"What are you talking about?" said
Marilla. "We're not in trouble."

"What are YOU talking about?" said
Dave. "That woman just yelled at us!"

"So what?" said Marilla.

"So that's getting in trouble," said
Dave.

"Um, no, it's not," said Marilla. "We're
OUT of trouble because we're walking

away from the woman and she has no idea who we are and we'll never see her again and we didn't do anything wrong anyway."

"I don't like getting yelled at."

Marilla stopped walking and made a big sigh. "Dave, you can't go through your whole life being afraid of getting yelled at. There are some people who will yell at you for anything. Some people just like to yell. You can't let them ruin your life . . . Right, Lyle?"

"Yeah," I said. Which doesn't sound like something amazing to say, but I really meant it because I had never thought about it like that before and I liked it. And I think Dave was sort of thinking it over too, because we started walking again and the argument was over.

The Qwikpick Adventure Society was a society again and ready for an adventure.

↑

Ms. Van Metre, our language arts teacher, had us pick from a list of tricks that authors use and look up the definition and find an example and then write our own. I picked "foreshadowing." That's when an author drops a big hint about what's going to happen later in the story . . . it's supposed to keep the reader interested.

The Qwikpick Adventure Society was a society again and ready for an adventure . . . We had no way of knowing it would be our last.

An easy way to foreshadow is to add a dot dot dot and "for now" to the end of a sentence. Dave and I came up with some examples . . .

# DOT DOT DOT JOKES
## by LYLE and DAVE

Jethro had finished vomiting...
FOR NOW.

TIMMY'S PRICELESS COLLECTION OF JEWEL-ENCRUSTED FABERGÉ EGGS WAS SAFE ... FOR NOW.

PORK RINDS WERE HARMLESS...

FOR NOW.

Spicy chili pork rind

LISTENING TO THE LION KING 5,000 TIMES HASN'T TURNED MARILLA INTO A DANGEROUS PSYCHOPATH...

FOR NOW.

THE POTTY-TRAINING SONGS THAT JEREMY'S PARENTS WERE PLAYING SEEMED TO BE WORKING GREAT...

FOR NOW.

End of Song

SUSIE'S FRIENDS WERE HAPPY!
SHE WASN'T SHOVELING POO ON THEM...

FOR NOW.

THE ABANDONED BASEMENT
SEEMED SAFE! NO ONE HAD
SEEN A RAT WITH A HUMAN FACE...

FOR NOW.

STEPHANIE HASN'T FALLEN
FACE-FIRST INTO COW MANURE...

FOR NOW.

THE CREEPY DOLL
WAS SMILING...

THESE ARE OUR
BEST DOT-DOT-
DOT JOKES...

FOR NOW.

FOR NOW.

Just to be clear, there are actually lots of Qwikpicks, but there are just two in Crickenburg— our Qwikpick and this other Qwikpick.

## SECTION XVI
## The Other Qwikpick

We got out of Elizabeth's neighborhood and back on North Franklin Street and kept walking. Soon we had to cross Main Street, which is where North Franklin Street turns into South Franklin Street.

"Hey, look!" I yelled. "It's the OTHER Qwikpick!"

"Have you ever been in there?" asked Marilla.

"No," I said. "We spend so much time at our Qwikpick that my parents never stop at this one."

"Honestly," said Dave, "I probably never would have been into ANY Qwikpick if it wasn't for you guys. My mother refuses to buy anything at a convenience store because they overcharge so much."

I was about to come to the Qwikpick's defense against this accusation of overcharging. It's one of Larry's favorite topics. He says that people think a convenience store OVERCHARGES and that you're paying extra for "the convenience." But he says that people only think that because they are used to buying stuff at giant grocery stores or Wal-Marts, which can UNDERCHARGE because they're selling in bulk.

But before I could get started, Marilla said, "Let's go in. Maybe they'll give us free drinks, like Larry does."

"We didn't bring our own cups," I said.

"Well, we still need to go in and see what it's like, right?"

So we went in.

Our Qwikpick is sort of like an old house or something that got turned into a convenience store. But this place was obviously built to be a convenience store. It was just sort of a box with windows.

It was weird because it was a lot of the same stuff, but all very neatly displayed. Too neat. And everything was too normal. They were missing the weird

old stuff and the wolf and Native
American figurines and stuff like
that.

And they didn't have a breakfast
area! No biscuits? Biscuits are
like the most important part of our
Qwikpick.

Then we looked at the second-most
important part: the chips aisle.

"Not much of a pork rind selection,"
said Marilla. "Just one brand. And
only regular and BBQ? Snore."

"Take a picture so we can show
Larry."

Marilla pulled out her camera and
that was when the yelling started.

"What do you think you're doing?"

It was an employee. A woman about
my mom's age and wearing the same
work uniform as my mom, but NOT like
my mom. This woman was furious.

"What are you taking that picture
for? What are you doing in here? Are
you buying or just snooping around?
Who did he say you're going to show
that picture to?"

"Uh, see, his parents work at the
other Qwikpick and--"

"Well, then why don't you go THERE
and bother THEM? I swear, there's a day
off of school and everybody thinks I'm a
babysitter. If you're buying something,
put that camera away and get out your
money. And if not then--oh, see? Now I've
got a line. I don't have any more time to
waste on this. Take your camera and go
home."

We left.

We were all sort of stunned and I
could tell Dave was upset about getting
yelled at for a second time, but Marilla
got us laughing again with a fake-out
that will go down in history as one of
the all-time great fake-outs: she turned
around and started walking back to the
store.

"Where are you going?" said me and
Dave at the same time. And frankly I
was worried that she was going back in
there to start yelling at that lady.
That's the sort of thing new Marilla
might do!

But then she said, "We forgot to ask for the free drinks."

I lost it. The idea of going back in there and asking the woman for a free drink after all that. I just started laughing so hard I could barely stand up. Dave was laughing too, but then he got worried the lady was going to see me "flopping around" in the parking lot and come out and yell at us.

"If she does, I'm definitely asking for the free drinks," said Marilla.

*And I almost believe she would!*

So after we settled down, we started walking down South Franklin again.

"Wow," I said. "I can't imagine my mom or dad or Larry yelling at kids that way, even if they stole something."

"I almost wish I HAD stolen something from her," said Marilla.

"What? You can't--"

"Dave, would you chill out? I obviously wouldn't! But I DID get a photo of the top secret pork rinds!"

"What was her deal? I mean, why

would anyone care about a picture of pork rinds?" asked Dave.

"Maybe she thought we were corporate spies, trying to steal the secret of her incredible pork rind success."

"Incredible Pork Rind Success: The Musical!"

"Everything's coming up bacon!"

"Pork secrets! Don't you go telling my . . . pork se-crets!"

After we ran out of pork rind lyrics, Dave said, "That makes me realize how lucky we are that Larry is such a nice guy and that your parents are cool, Lyle."

"Yeah," I said. "I guess what we learned is that there's no place like home."

"Somewhere . . . over the pork rinds," sang Dave, like it was still part of "Incredible Pork Rind Success: The Musical!"

↑

Normally, you would expect Marilla to jump in and sing the next line of a song like that. But she didn't. That's more foreshadowing, but I didn't catch it then either.

## SECTION XVII
## Other Stuff We Saw

The bad thing about walking along South Franklin Street is the noise. It's just whoosh whooosh whooosh RUUUMBLE the whole time because there's so much traffic. It's hard to figure out where all these people are going and why they didn't take the bypass if they're in such a big hurry.

The good thing about walking along South Franklin Street, though, is that you actually see stuff. Normally, in a car, everything is just sort of a blur, except for what's at the stoplights. The stuff in between just doesn't catch your eye unless it's the hot tub place with its creepy, rotting gorilla-in-a-hot-tub display.

When it takes you like two minutes to walk past an old building instead of two seconds, you see stuff that you've never seen before, even if you drive down South Franklin Street every day.

Here are some of the highlights. (Some of these things we saw before lunch and some after lunch, but I'm putting them all in this section just to keep things organized.)

* Two nasty old gloves alongside the road. They were about ten feet apart. But they were NOT a pair! One was a garden glove, and the other was a leather glove.

* A historical marker that said two colonial guys had fought a duel fifty feet from that spot. (So why didn't they put the marker ON the spot?) And Marilla asked: "Why is that worth a historical marker? If two guys get in a drunken brawl outside of the Dew Drop Inn today and one of them ends up dead, nobody puts up a historical marker."

* Lots of empty lots. Some had never been built on, and some had buildings that had been torn down. (Some had buildings that NEEDED to be torn

down.) Dave says his mom, who is a
Realtor, says these lots are impossible
to sell. They're so close to the road
that only a business would move there,
but any business that's moving wants
to be out at the bypass area, near Wal-
Mart and all that stuff. Same with
the old houses on North Franklin
(some of which are cool), which we saw
a bunch of. Dave says his mom says
that a hundred years ago they built
houses that could last a hundred
years or more, but the problem is that
a hundred years later no one wants
to live in them. So they have weird
businesses in them like mattress
stores, but now the mattress stores
want to move to the bypass too.

* Crab Creek. We crossed over Crab Creek
  on the bridge. I've never had a chance
  to look over the edge of the bridge
  before. It actually looks pretty cool
  down there. You see the railroad track
  and the creek. In this part of town,
  Crab Creek is pre-poop. (See official
  report #1 for all the pre- and post-
  poop details.)

* Lots of hair salons. Tanning salons too. The hair salons have crazy names like Stop! Scissor Time and Hair America. The tanning salons ALL have a picture of the sun wearing sunglasses.

* Shopping carts, everywhere. Down in the creek. Next to old buildings. In the middle of abandoned lots. One of the weirdest places was under a tractor trailer (which obviously didn't run). There were about twenty of them. Why?

Marilla thought it was so mysterious that it deserved a poem.

Huddled shopping carts

Did you seek each other out?

Or are you waiting for your store

To have a grand reopening?

Or are you happy where you are?

"You missed a great opportunity to rhyme 'shopping carts' with 'popping farts,'" said Dave, and Marilla punched him.

* Empty stores that you can't believe were ever stores. Like a place that sold organs. How many people needed to buy an organ even like fifty years ago, which is when it looks like this place was last open?

* Something my dad showed me. Back when Kroger was downtown, my dad would sometimes park, then take me for a walk before we went shopping. (That's when I saw the banana puree can-- see official report #1.) Something he showed me was still there, so I showed it to Marilla and Dave. It's a building that has a big ramp in the back that goes up to the roof. Dad said that when he was a kid--before the mall and Wal-Mart and everything was built--the place was a department store and you could park on the roof when you went shopping there.

"It would be cool to ride a bike up there," I said. "We could come back with our bikes and that could be a Qwikpick Adventure Society adventure."

"Or we could take our instruments up there and have a rooftop concert like the Beatles," said Dave.

"Lyle, you'll have to sing since you don't play an instrument," said Marilla.

"I don't know any Beatles songs."

"WHATTTT?????" said Dave. "You don't know ANY BEATLES SONGS????"

I'll cut it off there, but the next twenty minutes were Dave singing the title of every Beatles song he could think of and apparently there are about five hundred of them. Also we decided that going up on the roof would be really, really dumb. Marilla said if you dropped a Cheeto up there, the whole building would fall down.

## SECTION XVIII
## Time for Lunch!

We walked on and passed some more
stuff, including an actual log cabin.
Not sure if it had been there since log
cabin days or if someone had moved it
there so it would stand out from the other
businesses. Whatever it was, now it's a
tanning salon.

"We're almost to Hank's Hot and Cold!"
said Marilla.

"Oh yes!" I said. "I want some hot AND
some cold!"

"Uh," said Dave, "is that the place with
the big sign of a pig wearing sunglasses?"

"And mittens and a scarf!" I said.
"That's the place!"

"You've never been there?!?" asked
Marilla, genuinely shocked. "You're going
to LOVE it! It's the BEST barbecue in the
world!"

"Uh . . . I'm not eating there," said
Dave.

"She's not kidding," I said. "It's the

best restaurant in Crickenburg! And it's not just the barbecue, it's also the desserts! That's why they call it Hank's Hot AND Cold. They've got--"

"No, seriously, I can't eat there. Jews can't eat any kind of a pig."

"But you eat pork rinds at the Qwikpick."

"No, I don't."

"Yes, you do."

"Dude, I think I know what I eat. Even if I wasn't Jewish, I wouldn't eat a pork rind."

"You eat chicken, right? I've seen you eat like eight servings of nuggets."

"Yes, but not eight--"

"Well, just order some barbecue chicken, then."

"They have chicken? It looks like all pigs to me."

By this time, we were close enough to see Hank's in its full glory. And Dave was right--it was pretty piggy. In addition to the big sign, there are pig murals on the outside of the building

and a neon pig in the window. And the
biggest pig of all is the Pig Van, with
pig ears on top.

"See? Pig, pig, pig, pig . . . . ."

"I promise you two things: they have
chicken and you're going to love it.
Come ON!"

I don't want to turn the report into
a restaurant review, so I'm going to
sum it up.

* The BBQ was fantastic and Dave
  did love it. (We all got chicken,
  just to make him happy.)

* You can eat inside or outside, but
  we decided to eat inside since it
  was air-conditioned and because
  Dave said, "Who wants to eat right
  next to the road?"

* There were five bottles of
  different flavor sauces on every
  table. Marilla explained how
  each kind comes from a different
  part of North Carolina, South

Carolina, or Tennessee. Virginia
doesn't have a famous sauce yet, said
Marilla, but Hank's Sweet Red (the
not-secret secret ingredient: root
beer) deserves to be it. I agree with
her.

* There is also a whole roll of paper
  towels on every table because it's
  very messy.

* Dave ordered a side of green beans
  instead of fries. They came with
  a huge chunk of pork floating in
  them, so he couldn't eat them. "You
  should have ordered the FRIED green
  beans," said Marilla.

* There were about fifty different
  T-shirts for sale, one of which
  Marilla said was X-rated, but
  Dave and I couldn't figure it out.
  Another of them was pretty gross.
  It was a pig with a halo saying,
  "Thanks for having me for lunch!"

\* Marilla wanted all three of us
to buy T-shirts that said "Best
Friends" and had a picture of a
pig, a hamburger bun, and a bottle
of sauce. But Dave whispered,
"That would be evidence directly
linking us to the crime we're about
to commit." And he was right, so we
didn't get the shirts. (Plus they
cost too much anyway.)

Ears!

The Pig Van!

# SECTION XIX
## Tiger's Blood

"Oh, man," Marilla said. "I am so full of HOT, I don't know if I have room for COLD. Ug."

"You mean, the soft-serve ice cream?" said Dave. "I'm not really into soft-serve. Maybe we can stop somewhere and get real ice cream."

"Whoa!" I said. "First of all, soft-serve rocks. And second of all, this isn't just any soft-serve we're talking about. This is the Tiger's Blood Sundae!"

"Ug," said Dave.

"You've actually ordered that?" Marilla said to me.

"WHAT??? You come here all the time and you've never had the Tiger's Blood Sundae?"

"No, I usually get the Brownie Boogie."

"Okay," I said, "the Brownie Boogie is pretty good. But wait until you try the Tiger's Blood Sundae."

"Uh, I'll wait about a hundred years, if you don't mind," said Dave.

"No, you're going to love it! Let me explain," I said. "It's not an ice cream flavor. It's something more awesome than that by like 100,000,000 miles. It's soft-serve AND shaved ice together! A little bit of soft-serve vanilla on the bottom and then a layer of Tiger's Blood shaved ice, and then more soft-serve, and then--"

"Okay," said Dave. "Don't say 'more Tiger's Blood,' because that's a concept I never thought I would ever hear and definitely never want to hear again."

"Okay," I said. "But you realize that Tiger's Blood is not actual blood from a tiger, right? It's a flavor."

"So it's like artificial flavor? I don't get it. Don't they have like cherry or lemon, or is everything blood-and-guts stuff like that?" asked Dave.

"Yeah, they've got all the boring flavors, but you can get those anywhere. This is--you know--the thing. This is the thing to get at Hank's. Trust me, it's awesome! I ALWAYS get a Tiger's Blood Sundae!"

"I never would've thought of you as a Tiger's Blood kind of guy," said Marilla.

"Yeah," said Dave. "I can't really picture you walking up and saying 'Give me some Tiger's Blood, lady.'"

"Give Me Some Tiger's Blood, Lady: The Musical!" said Marilla. "I want something that's sticky-sweet, Red and thick as mud! So, hey, pretty lady . . . Serve me up some of that Tiiiii-gerrrrrr's Blood."

"Okay," I said, "you guys can laugh about it now, but after you've tasted it you'll be like 'I will order this no matter how embarrassing it may be.'"

"Well," said Dave, "as much as I would LOVE to try it, I think we need to go. We're still not sure exactly how long it will take to walk down there and (whisper) find the tomb, so we need to move along."

"Okay," I said. "We can stop on the way back."

"Well," said Dave, "we weren't really going to come back this way. I was planning to--"

"We ARE stopping here on the way back," I said. "And you guys are going to thank me!"

Dave always tries to be the boss of directions and I know he has everything mapped out, but come on, man! A Tiger's Blood Sundae!

# SECTION XX
## Construction Zone

After that, we kept walking. We went under the bypass, which was weird and not very pedestrian-friendly.

Then we passed a sign that said "Entering Montgomery County. Regional Economic GlobalSpark Development Zone."

"What does that mean?" I asked.

"I guess it means it's easier to build a new building in the county than in the city, because look at all the construction," Dave explained.

Up ahead there were a few older (or at least not brand-new) buildings, but there were several that were brand-new and some more that weren't even finished. There was a big metal sign wired to the fence outside one that said "Future Site of Crickenburg Urology Associates."

"I wonder what--," I started.

"You DON'T want to know!" said Dave.

"One of my brothers had to go to a urologist once after a soccer injury. You wouldn't even begin to believe the stuff on the pamphlets in the waiting room!"

"You Wouldn't Even Begin to Believe the Stuff on the Pamphlets in the Waiting Room: The Musical!" yelled Marilla.

"Don't sing about that! Whatever you do, don't start singing about it!" said Dave.

"So it's urology, like urine or--," I started to ask.

"YES! It is. Let's not even start talking about it. Ug. Uck. Yayayayaya. Happy thoughts. Happy thoughts!"

Unfortunately, right then the sidewalk ended.

"Where the sidewalks ends!" yelled Marilla.

"Uh, yeah," said Dave.

"Like the book."

"What book?"

"WHAAT???" yelled Marilla. "You never

read <u>Where the Sidewalk Ends</u>? Shel
Silverstein????"

"Somebody wrote a novel about the
end of the sidewalk?"

"It's not a novel, it's a book of
poems."

"Poems???" yukked Dave. "What kind
of an idiot would write poems about the
end of the sidewalk?"

"Well, you once wrote a poem about a
poop fountain," I reminded him.

"True," said Dave. "I stand corrected.
I will read this poem and I'm sure I
will enjoy it very much."

This may sound like Dave and Marilla fighting all over again, like at the beginning of the trip. But this is actually a good kind of fighting. Dave loves to argue, so if you know that ahead of time and just argue with him for fun, then sometimes it can be entertaining. Of course, sometimes it can also be unbelievably annoying.

"ARRGH!" said Marilla.
"What? I said I'd enjoy it!"
"You are infuriating!"

So now we had to walk right next to the chain-link fence, basically on the shoulder of the road.

"Nice . . . ," said Dave. "Walking through gravel, broken glass, and cigarette butts and about to be run over by a truck."

He wasn't kidding about any of that. Having a truck go right past you is not pleasant. First of all, they're going really fast here. Second of all, they don't move an inch out of their way for you. And third of all, right after they pass you, you get hit by this blast of air that almost knocks you backward and then almost sucks you into the road.

Luckily, we soon got to a place where the shoulder was wider and there was no construction fence. But there was still a lot of construction. I mean a LOT of construction.

They were building a whole neighborhood at the next construction site, and when you looked back there, it was those skinny two-story houses that are all pushed up against each other.

A really nice sign said "Regency Courte Townhomes, Starting in the Low 120s."

"What are the low 120s?"

"That means $120,000," said Dave. "But what it really means is that most of the houses cost a lot more than that. My mom says they'll offer to build you a house for $120,000, but then there's all this other stuff, like extra bathrooms or better windows, that get added on and it ends up costing a lot more. Like maybe $200,000."

"Wow, that's a lot of money," I said.

"Yeah, especially to live next door to

Urology Associates!" said Dave. "Having
to think about what's going on inside
that building all the time! Yuck!!!"

"Hey, Marilla, aren't you going to
make fun of the name?" I asked. "It's
got that extra 'e' on 'Court' that you
like."

"Actually, I have something to tell
you guys about Ye Olde Regency Courte
on the way back. But right now let's go
and find the plantation."

So we kept walking and passed more
construction. And then we passed
someone's house. A really nice little
normal house, maybe even an antique,
with a driveway and everything.
Completely surrounded by construction
and stuff. There was a "For Sale" sign
in the front yard.

For Sale
Valley Realtors . . . the friendly
experts!
2.3 Acr. Zoned C3
Call Linda Raskin or Cindy
Quesenberry, etc.

"Oh geez!" said Dave. "This is one of my mom's properties. Let's move it out!"

And he started walking real fast, so Marilla and I had to walk real fast to catch up with him. And then we could see the Kmart construction site up ahead and . . . a flying Porta-Potty!

# SECTION XXI
## The Flying Porta-Potty

Okay, we soon realized that it wasn't flying. It was hanging at an angle from a long cable that was hanging from a big crane. But it was like 50 feet in the air and kind of twisting around in the breeze.

We were all like "What?????"

"Uh, why is there a Porta-Potty hanging in the air?" said Dave.

"I have no idea," Marilla said.

"I do!" I said. "What if one of the construction workers went into the Porta-Potty and had like massive explosive diarrhea? And then the smell was so bad that all the other construction workers couldn't breathe, so the crane guy lifted it up out of smell range?"

"And what if," said Marilla, "the guy was still in it when they lifted it up there . . . and he's still up there, trapped with the stink?"

"Wouldn't he open the door?" asked Dave.

"If I was in a Porta-Potty five hundred

feet in the air, I'd keep the door closed no matter how bad it smelled so I didn't fall out," I said.

"Five hundred? More like fifty," said Dave.

"I've got another theory," said Marilla and in fact we came up with a bunch of other theories.

Other possible theories:

* It's a special Porta-Potty for flying superheroes.
* It only looks like a Porta-Potty, but it's actually a time machine, kind of like the telephone-booth time machine in this leftover Qwikpick video we watched called <u>Bill and Ted's Bogus Journey</u>. (Apparently it was a sequel to another movie, but that one must have been better because (a) I guess someone bought it and (b) it couldn't have been worse.)
* The construction crews lift the Porta-Potties up at night so that kids don't tip them over. (This theory is so boring, it's probably the true one.)

By this time we were past the Kmart construction site (which we could tell was definitely the Kmart construction site because they had already delivered the giant "K" for the front of the building.) We were walking past a sort of like really cruddy woods. Not like a nice place, but more like bushes and trash and thorns and kind of weedy-looking trees.

"We must be getting near the plantation," said Dave.

But when we got past the bushes, we came to this big area that had been totally bulldozed. It was just a big flat dirt field. Really big! There was a "For Sale" sign here too.

This is the sort of place that gets my dad fired up. You see places like this around Crickenburg all the time now and my dad always starts fussing like this: "Why would they bulldoze it BEFORE they sell it? Maybe someone would like to buy it BECAUSE it's got hills and grass and trees. Too late now!!! Bunch of greedy idiots!"

"The old ladies said the Kmart was going to be right next to the plantation," said Marilla. "So maybe it's back there in all those weeds and stuff?"

So we turned around and looked at the woods place, and way, way, way back in the bushes and trees we saw a chimney sticking up. An old crumbly-looking chimney.

"That must be it!"

Since there was no one around, we snuck across the bulldozed lot until we were back as far as the chimney. Then we just needed to push through maybe one hundred feet of weeds and stuff to get to the actual place.

# SECTION XXII
## Ow!

"Ow!" said Marilla.

"Ow!" said Dave.

"Ow!" said me.

MANY TIMES EACH!!!!

We were all wearing T-shirts and shorts and the thorns either stuck in our clothes or scratched our arms and legs . . . and in Dave's case got caught in his hair.

"How come every one of our adventures involves physical discomfort?" Dave asked.

"How come every one of our adventures involves poop?" I asked.

"How come every one of our adventures involves me being slowed down by a couple of whiny wimps?" asked Marilla.

She didn't really mean that!

# SECTION XXIII
## The Plantation Manor

Even an official report can skip
over stuff when that stuff is really
boring, so I'm not going to write up
all the rest of the trouble we had
getting through the weeds and junk.
And I mean JUNK! Not Civil War junk
either but like . . . junk from maybe
fifty years ago. Boring junk too.
So I'm skipping straight to when we
finally got to the "mansion."

    "This is a mansion?" said Dave.
"What a dump."

"I guess it was nice two hundred years ago," I said. "This must have been a pretty big house for back then."

"Well, I can see why those crazy ladies are going around trying to get children to give them money," said Marilla. "They're going to need a fortune to turn this place into a museum or whatever."

We looked in through a window.

"Make that a triple fortune!"

Inside it was empty and there were boards missing in the floor and holes in the walls.

We probably could have figured out a way to get inside--most of the windows were busted--but honestly we didn't want to. It looked like the whole place would fall over on us.

"It's too bad Sherman didn't burn this place down," said Marilla.

"Sherman who?" I asked.

"Duh. Didn't you pay any attention last year in history class?" asked Dave with that tone of his. "Sherman was the Union general who went through the South burning everything down to weaken the Confederacy."

"Oh, that guy," I said, even though I had never heard of him.

"Well, he missed this place!"

"Marilla, you are cold. You seriously wish he had burned down MORE of Virginia?" said Dave.

"Uh, the house of a slave master? Yes! I knew you guys were going to go soft on me."

"I didn't say anything!" I said.

"And I haven't gone soft," argued Dave.

"All right, I shouldn't have said 'soft,'" said Marilla. "But if you knew what plantations were like, you'd probably wish Sherman had burned more down too."

"I know what they were like," said Dave. "We did a whole unit on the Civil War!"

"Yeah, but that barely even got into it. Wait until you hear this."

She pulled a book out of her backpack.

"I brought this along because I knew I would need to get you guys fired up to complete the mission."

She showed us the cover. It was called <u>Twenty-Two Years a Slave, and Forty Years a Freeman</u>. "My grandmother gave it to me a couple of years ago. I've never been able to finish it. It's too much. But like I said, it's just what we all need to get fired up for going to knock the guy down . . . This is from page one."

ATTENTION: ALERT! READ THIS!
DON'T GO ANY FURTHER UNTIL YOU READ THIS!

We, The Qwikpick Adventure Society, feel like we need to warn you before you go any further.

We don't know who you are or why you are reading our top secret report, but since you are reading it, we want to make sure you are prepared for what comes next.

So far, you've read some stuff that seemed really intense to us because it happened to us, but none of it is like what Marilla reads out of that book. In fact, we want to give you the option of just skipping it if you don't think you can handle it. Just skip to the next section. The main thing you need to know is that slavery is really, really, really, really, really bad, and, in fact, it's even worse than you think, and when Dave and I heard what Marilla read, we DID get fired up just like she said.

You know, even though we're saying that you can skip it, maybe you SHOULD read it. Maybe you think you know what slavery was like. I had seen slaves in a couple of movies and it always looked like their clothes were raggedy and their lives were pretty bad . . . but I never knew it was THIS bad!

Okay, if you're sure . . . Here is
what Marilla read.

"The overseer always went around
with a whip, about nine feet long,
made of the toughest kind of
cowhide, the but-end of which was
loaded with lead . . .

This made a dreadful instrument
of torture, and, when in the hands
of a cruel overseer, it was truly
fearful. With it, the skin of an ox
or a horse could be cut through . . .

Thirty-nine was the number of
lashes ordinarily inflicted for the
most trifling offence . . .

The slave husband must submit
without a murmur, to see the form of
his cherished, but wretched wife,
not only exposed to the rude gaze
of a beastly tyrant, but he must
unresistingly see the heavy cowhide
descend upon her shrinking flesh,
and her manacled limbs writhe in
inexpressible torture, while her
piteous cries for help ring through
his ears unanswered."

Marilla is right—it's hard not to cuss when you're talking about something like this.

"*#@$!" I said. "That's enough for me. Let's go find the guy and kick him over!"

But Dave had to be skeptical, as always.

"Maybe that kind of stuff wasn't going on around here. That's like stuff from the Deep South."

"No, the writer, Austin Steward, was a slave right here IN VIRGINIA. This could have happened right at this house, on this farm."

"But—"

"I know you don't want to believe it's true, but it is. This could have been my great-great-great-grandmother."

And then Dave was quiet a minute. "All right, then," he said suddenly. "For your great-great-great-grandmother and all the slaves here AND in ancient Egypt . . . Let's go kick the #$&* down!"

For the first time ever? I mean, he was really thinking.

Man, it was weird hearing Dave cuss!

# SECTION XXIV
## The $*&*@'s Tomb

We were so fired up, we charged
into the bushes and went around back
looking for the tomb. Yes, we got
scraped and stuck and scratched, but
it would be REALLY wimpy to whine
about that stuff right after hearing
about people getting whipped like
that.

But I did yelp when I tripped on
a rock. But it wasn't just a rock. It
turned out to be a little gravestone
lying flat on the ground. You could
see that there had been words on it a
long time ago, but you couldn't really
read them now.

So then we noticed more flat stones
and realized we must be in the family
burial plot that the Greenhill ladies
had been talking about.

And then we saw the tomb. I don't
know what you think a tomb looks like,
but you MUST have imagined something
more interesting than this.

It was just a big stone box that stuck up maybe three feet out of the ground. At one end there was a hole in the ground . . . completely filled up with weeds, thorns, and, believe it or not, a small tree. Sort of down in that hole was a steel door that went into the stone box.

It would have been seriously difficult to get down in there and open the door, but we didn't have to. A big section of the top of the box had fallen in a long time ago.

We had to scrape through more thorns, but we got right up next to it and looked through the big hole in the roof and down into, well, a big hole in the ground.

Guess what was in there?

If you guessed more weeds, you're right.

If you guessed a bunch of chunks of rock from when the roof collapsed, you're right.

If you guessed a standing-up corpse, you're wrong.

"He's gone!" I said.

"Probably he's down there under all those rocks!" said Dave.

He got out a flashlight and tried to shine it into all the dark places.

I got a long stick and tried to use it to move some of the rocks that were down there.

We saw some stuff that maybe looked like bones . . . maybe.

"I guess we'll have to crawl down in there," I said.

"Maybe" is the official word that Dave and I agreed on for this report. But for me personally, I know what I saw: bones!

This wasn't even me trying to be brave to impress Marilla. (Although I had completely prepared myself to do just about anything to impress Marilla.) The thought of sneaking into a dark tomb had been scary. Hopping over this wall to move a few rocks around didn't seem scary at all. And as far as a ghost? No way. A snake maybe, but not a ghost.

"Don't bother," said Marilla.

Dave and I were like, "HUH?"

"What are you going to do? Find all the pieces, put him together, and then kick him over again?"

"We've got to do something!" I said. "What about two hundred-year-old justice?"

"You know," said Marilla, "in some ways it seems like justice has already been done. I mean, if he had just been buried normally, he'd be lying down comfortably under one of those flat rocks, but because he was the world's biggest &@$& and had to have this special standing-up tomb, he's now been crushed under his own gravestone and has a blackberry bush growing out of him."

"Note to self," said Dave, "don't eat the blackberries."

"So we're just going to turn around and go home?" I asked. "This will be the worst Qwikpick Adventure Society adventure of all time if we don't do SOMETHING! I mean, we walked three miles to get here. We can't just walk away."

"Don't worry," said Marilla with this crazy smile all of a sudden.

"I AM going to do something," she said. "I AM going to lay down some justice. This guy's body is at the bottom of a hole in the ground in a weed jungle next to a Kmart. But he STILL deserves worse. And I'm going to take care of it . . . But you guys will have to walk away first."

"What? Why?"

"Because," said Marilla, "I'm going to pee on him."

The Tomb

# SECTION XXV
## Did She Really Do It?

"Did you really do it?"

"Did you REALLY do it?"

"You actually unzipped and peed down in that hole?"

"A lady never talks about unzipping," said Marilla.

"Well, most ladies don't go around peeing on corpses," said Dave. "Not that I'm criticizing. I think it's awesome, I just can't believe you REALLY did it!"

"Well, I did. You're welcome to go back and look for pee stains on the bones if you need to."

"Pee Stains on the Bones: The Musical!" I said.

"This is bigger than fake show tunes," said Dave. "And WAY bigger than haiku. I think we need to compose one of those epic ballads like a bard would sing in Valhalla."

"Where's Valhalla?"

"You don't know what Valhalla is? Valhalla is like heaven for the Norse

gods like Thor and Odin, and if you're
a really great warrior, you get to go
there and drink mead, and if you're
a really, really great warrior, you go
there, drink mead, AND they sing a song
about you, like, 'Mighty Frodo did smite
the dragon and chopt off its head.'"

"First of all, you're confusing Frodo
with Bilbo," said Marilla. "And neither
of them is a Norse warrior anyway."

"Fine, we won't write an epic ballad
about you, then," said Dave.

But he was too late because I already
had the first few lines:

> "Marilla, the lovely maiden,
> Didst walkest many a mile,
> With her handsome helper,
> The one they call Sir Lyle."

"What about me."

"And also Dave."

"Great, thanks," said Dave.
All this was going on while we were

walking back from the plantation/ Kmart area.

"Oh, yeah," I said as we passed the Regency Courte town houses. "What were you going to tell us about this place, Marilla?"

"Ug . . . just hold on until we get back to Hank's," she said. "Right now I think you guys better finish my epic ballad."

This is one of those things where everything seems perfect and you're just walking along thinking everything is perfect and you have no idea that it's really not perfect at all and everything is about to fall apart, but you don't know it. I wish it had been fifty miles from the Kmart to Hank's.

The Epic Ballad of Marilla
the Awesome

Marilla, the lovely maiden,
Didst walketh many a mile,
With her handsome helper,
The one they call Sir Lyle.
And also Dave . . .
And also Dave.

"Come with me to topple
The long-dead slave master!"
"Why should we do this?"
Lyle he diddith ask her.
And also Dave . . .
And also Dave.

She said, "We must do what
His mistreated slaves couldeth not.
We will sneak down there
And kick his bony butt.
To the bottom of his grave . . .
To the bottom of his grave."

But uponeth our arrival,
His butt couldeth not be found.
So Marilla she did squat . . .
And her pee raineth down.
On his grave . . .
On his grave.

Now the slaver lies down at last
With salty pee for a pillow!
Justice has been done at last . . .
By the awesome one, Marilla!
And Lyle and Dave . . .
And Lyle and Dave!

# SECTION XXVI
## Tiger's Blood II

When we got back to Hank's we were
all hot and thirsty and ready for the
soft-serve. Instead of going inside, we
walked up to the ice-cream-only window.

I got a Tiger's Blood Sundae and Dave
surprised me by ordering one, too.

"How can I NOT order Tiger's Blood
when I just came from dispensing two
hundred-year-overdue justice?" said
Dave. "I would drink REAL tiger's blood
if they had it . . . Not really."

Marilla ordered this thing called
the Dirt Dessert, which has gummy worms
and chocolate crumb "dirt." She also got
a cookie and stuck it in there to look
like a grave.

"A toast!" said Marilla after we
carried our stuff to a picnic table. "A
toast to The Qwikpick Adventure Society!
Remember in the very first official
report Lyle wrote that we weren't going
to fight an ancient evil? Well, we sort
of did. AND we kicked its *#&@!"

"Or at least we peed on its bony dust," said Dave.

"WE PEED ON ITS BONY DUST: THE MUSICAL!" Marilla and I both said at once. And we all clinked our glasses--except that they were actually plastic cups.

Then we all took a big bite and Marilla said, "This is the most disgusting thing I've ever put in my mouth."

And Dave said, "You should have gotten the Tiger's Blood."

I told her she could share mine.

She tried it. Then she said, "Yeah, you're right. It's good."

Then she said, "I'm moving."

"WHAT???"

"WHERE???"

"To those town houses. My stepdad's on disability now and my parents have been saving up the checks to make a down payment."

Marilla looked at me and it was a certain look and I knew exactly what she meant, but I can't explain it. It

meant a lot of things about how she
was sorry to leave and sorry that I
was staying and that I was one of the
reasons why her parents wanted to
move out of the trailer park. That her
parents thought their family didn't
belong in a trailer park where their
daughter would have to hang around
with someone like me who does belong
in a trailer park.

"I'm sorry, Lyle," she said. "They
never planned for us to stay, and
then after the rat thing happened,
they started talking about moving
right away."

"Right away? When are you moving?"

"This week. As soon as school is out.
My uncle is bringing his truck over to
help us move."

I was already feeling lonely
thinking that Marilla wouldn't be
in the trailer park anymore, but
Dave, being map-minded and all, had
already realized that it was even
worse than this. WAY WORSE!

"When we passed the Crickenburg
town limits sign . . . That was before

we got to the town houses, wasn't it?" he asked.

"Yes," said Marilla.

"So if the townhouses are in the county, then . . . you'll be going to the OTHER middle school?"

"Yes. North Fork Middle School."

"Crap. Band is going to suck without you."

"BAND?" I shouted. "My whole LIFE is going to suck!"

"Mine too," said Marilla. "But just for a year! We'll all be going to Crickenburg High School together!"

UNOFFICIAL personal note

I thought for a while about putting the crying into the official report. But it was too hard to explain all the reasons why I started crying. And if I left those out, then it would just say, "I, Lyle, started crying," and that would make it sound like I was just being a big baby.

But actually it was a lot more than that. Yes, part of it was realizing that I was going to be all alone at Crab Creek Estates now. I couldn't even walk past Marilla's trailer and wave anymore.

But some of it was like relief crying—you know, like when everybody thinks somebody is going to die and then they don't.

When I said, "My whole life is going to suck," I wasn't even thinking about my WHOLE life, like the future. I was just thinking about mostly this coming summer and maybe a little bit about 8th grade. But as soon as Marilla said, "high school," I realized how close I had come to losing her forever. If her parents had picked town houses closer to Salem or something, then she WOULD be at a different high school and I might never see her again.

So I was actually crying partly because I was sad about what WAS happening and partly because I was happy about what might have happened but WASN'T.

And then I realized that even though we'd be together at school again . . . we'd probably never be together at the Qwikpick again. I had always figured her parents would relax a bit and let her hang out with me again, eventually.

But that was never going to happen now.

All of it—the Ms. Pac-Man, the old records, the broken TV, the leftover biscuits, the just sitting around cracking up about dumb stuff, The Qwikpick Adventure Society, the official reports—it was all over.

Dave had figured that out too. And even though he wasn't crying like me, he was pretty mad.

"Your parents have just destroyed
The Qwikpick Adventure Society
forever! It was bad enough when they
grounded you and ruined the last
couple of months, but now they're
making it permanent! This is *&*#$!%
stupid!"

Marilla and I just about fell over.
Dave, who had never cussed in his
whole life before he said #$&* earlier,
had now dropped the biggest-possible
cuss word.

I looked around to see if anybody
had heard him. Luckily we were still
the only customers.

"Okay . . . ," said Marilla. "Now,
settle down for a minute. So, listen
. . . Yes, this probably does mean I
won't be hanging around the Qwikpick
much."

"Ever," I said.

"Okay, maybe not ever," said
Marilla. "BUT that's the reason why
I wanted to come here. This place
is about halfway between Crab
Creek Estates and Regency Courte
Townhomes, right?"

"Well, actually--"

"Yes!" I said. "Close enough! Are you saying we can meet here?"

"Yes . . . ," said Marilla. "I THINK so. I'll have to see how the grounding thing works out with my parents. It was one thing to break the rules today so that we could deliver two-hundred-year-overdue justice, but I'm going to need to be a good little girl again for a while. But then I think my parents are going to ease up on the grounding and then I'll be able to walk downtown and get a Tiger's Blood Sundae . . . And if you also just happen to be downtown getting a Tiger's Blood Sundae, then that would be awesome."

"And," said Dave, "if one of us gets here, but the others don't, we can leave them a note on the community bulletin board--using our code names, of course!"

Not as awesome as hanging out at the Qwikpick, but, yes, it would be awesome.

"Oh great," said Marilla. "Dear Gorilla, Sorry I missed you, Sincerely, Croco-Lyle and the Kung Fu Jew."

And that was officially the last thing The Qwikpick Adventure Society ever laughed about.

We walked back to Elizabeth's to drop off Marilla and get our bikes. (Marilla went inside to tell Elizabeth why today had been so important and that she was leaving school and all that, and I imagine they made up and became friends again, etc.)

And that was officially the last thing The Qwikpick Adventure Society ever did.

Actually, before Marilla went into Elizabeth's, she whispered something in my ear. "Don't worry, Lyle. Haven't you ever heard of a long-distance love affair?" Since Dave was right there, I didn't think anything more was going to happen than a half-hug, and just hearing the word "love" would have been enough to make everything worth it by 1,000,000 miles. But then Marilla yelled, "Look away, Dave!" And . . . she kissed me. It was quick, but it was also amazing.

And then Dave and I rode our bikes back to his house and he asked me if I wanted to stay, but I said I would go back to the Qwikpick and start writing up the official report.

And I started riding home, but then I remembered I still had the wreath. So I stopped at the cemetery that's on the hill across from Mountain View Pointe and left it there at a grave that had some flags on it. I stood there for a few minutes and thought about stuff. And THEN I rode back to the Qwikpick and started writing up this report.

And THAT was officially the end of The Qwikpick Adventure Society . . .

We, the former members of THE
QWIKPICK ADVENTURE SOCIETY, do
solemnly swear that this was a true
and faithful account of our trip to
kick a corpse (which turned into doing
something else to a corpse).


Lyle Hertzog


Marilla Anderson


David H. Raskin

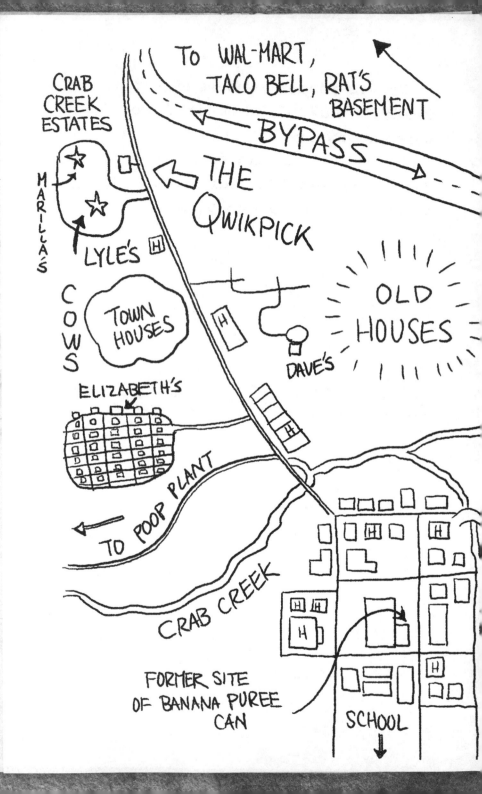

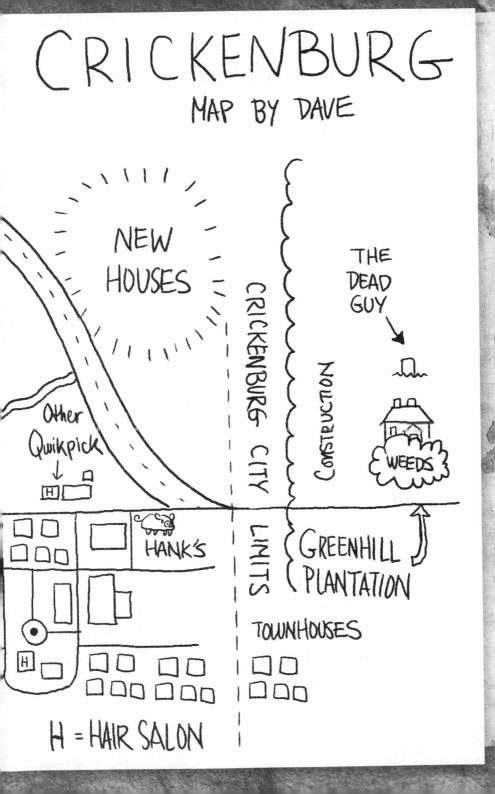

Another note to the reader from Tom Angleberger

As you can imagine, this official report left me with a lot of questions.

Did Lyle and his friends REALLY do these things? I mean, the pictures prove that they went to these places, but did Marilla REALLY pee on the slave master? (I personally believe she did, but as a reporter I like to have confirmation.)

Why did they leave the reports at the Qwikpick?

And was it REALLY the end?

I actually called up the guy who had given me the papers in the first place. I asked him if I could stop by the Qwikpick and look around to see if I could find anything else that would tell me what happened.

"I guess you haven't driven down South Franklin Street lately," he said. "It's gone."

"What's gone?"

"That old building. We're already building the new Qwikpick."

The next day, I drove by to take a look. He wasn't kidding. The Qwikpick is long gone. The new one looks like it's going to be just your basic boring convenience store. While I was there, I drove through Crab Creek Estates. I'm not even sure what I was looking for. I probably wouldn't have recognized Lyle even if I had driven right past him. But I didn't see ANYBODY, except a woman who might have been Jennifer from the Green Trailer.

So I was about to try Googling their names, but that just didn't feel right. There would be absolutely no mystery left. I would have all the answers . . . and the answers might turn out to be different from the ones I hoped they would be.

So I went back and read all the reports again, looking for some kind of clues. Nothing!

But then I remembered that when I had sorted through the three reports—which was a huge job because they were all mixed up—I had found a few things that just didn't seem to fit anywhere.

These included some of Dave's sketches for zombie characters, a piece of paper on which the word "EARWIG" had been drawn in extremely fancy letters with all sort of flourishes and waving banners, and the following list.

At first I thought they were possible names for rock bands, but now I realize that it holds the answers I wanted. Not EVERY answer, of course, and in fact it raises some new questions. Like: who is the fourth person mentioned? But it gives me just enough answers so that I can rest easy knowing it wasn't "the end" after all.

The Crickenburgers

Crickenburgers with Cheese--vetoed
by Dave because of the kosher
thing about meat and dairy

Crickenburgers with
Special Sauce

The Beatles--I can't explain it,
but when Dave suggested this, we
all laughed our heads off.

M.E.L.D.

D.E.L.M.

Crab Creek Critters

The Society Formerly Known as The
Qwikpick Adventure Society

The Crypt Kicker Five--No one liked
this because we're four instead of
five, but Dave REFUSED to change
it because it's from some old song.

The Hoopy Froods

The All-Zombie Marching Band
(featuring Lyle)

The Origami Pegasus
Disaster Squad

THE ORIGAMI PEGASUS
DISASTER SQUAD

The Molly Hatchett
Fan Club

Larry's Leftover Biscuit Eaters--Dave
didn't like this one because he said
it sounded like WE were leftovers. So
then Marilla suggested . . .

Larry's Leftovers--which
was the favorite for
a while until we came up
with this.

LARRY'S LEFTOVERS

The Tiger's Blood
Tasting Committee

UNANIMOUSLY
APPROVED!!!!!!!!!!!

THE TIGER'S BLOOD
TASTING COMMITTEE

So many people believed in the Qwikpick and helped us publish these official reports. But there was one person who was determined to see the story told all the way to the end. So this final report is dedicated to Susan Van Metre. Even better, Larry is planning to name a breakfast biscuit after her!
—T.A.

The illustrations in this book are by Jen Wang.
The photographs are by Tom Angleberger.

The excerpt on page 127 is from *Twenty-Two Years a Slave, and Forty Years a Freeman*, a memoir by Austin Steward, published in 1857.

PUBLISHER'S NOTE: This is a work of fiction. Names, characters, places, and incidents are either the product of the author's imagination or are used fictitiously, and any resemblance to actual persons, living or dead, business establishments, events, or locales is entirely coincidental.

Cataloging-in-Publication Data has been applied for and may be obtained from the Library of Congress.

ISBN: 978-1-4197-1906-6

Text copyright © 2016 Tom Angleberger
Illustrations copyright © 2016 Jen Wang
Book design by Pamela Notarantonio

Published in 2016 by Amulet Books, an imprint of ABRAMS. All rights reserved. No portion of this book may be reproduced, stored in a retrieval system, or transmitted in any form or by any means, mechanical, electronic, photocopying, recording, or otherwise, without written permission from the publisher.

Amulet Books and Amulet Paperbacks are registered trademarks of Harry N. Abrams, Inc.

Printed and bound in U.S.A.
10 9 8 7 6 5 4 3 2 1

Amulet Books are available at special discounts when purchased in quantity for premiums and promotions as well as fundraising or educational use. Special editions can also be created to specification. For details, contact specialsales@abramsbooks.com or the address below.

ABRAMS
THE ART OF BOOKS SINCE 1949
115 West 18th Street
New York, NY 10011
www.abramsbooks.com